Date Night on Union Station

Book One of EarthCent Ambassador

Date Night on Union Station

Paradise Pond Press

ISBN 0-9723801-9-1

Copyright 2014 by E. M. Foner

Northampton, Massachusetts

One

"In conclusion, it is the view of Union Station Consulate that the trade in counterfeit Earth chess sets has not been impacted by enforcement activities, and perversely, the crackdown has forced the principal actors to master molecular tagging, thus accelerating their technical competency and leading to increasingly sophisticated forgeries of other high value exports, especially playing cards and kitchen gadgets."

Kelly grimaced at the length of her last sentence. Perhaps it needed a few more commas or another period? But she suspected that the transcription program wrote better English than she spoke, so she decided to leave well enough alone. The report to EarthCent concluded her Friday afternoon ritual of taking stock in the week, even though she knew from experience that some diplomats flooded EarthCent with multiple missives a day, while others preferred to lay low unless something was going very wrong.

"Are you going to go home and get ready for your date now, or do I have to tell the girls to come and drag you?" asked Donna, the office manager for the consulate. Donna had accepted a post as the office gopher when she was still a teenager, but quickly grew disillusioned with the

1

romance of living in space when she realized that the employees of the recently established consulate never took a day off from work.

In a display of innate executive potential, Donna convinced Gryph, the Stryx intelligence who ran Union Station, to begin operating the corridor lights of the human sections on a 24 hour cycle. Then she counted five days and declared a weekend. The two hundred thousand plus Earth expatriates living on the station at the time assumed this was another mysterious decision of the Stryx, and they settled into the new schedule with no more than the usual complaining.

"I'm going, I'm going," Kelly replied, and pushed back from the display table that served as her desk. "I only received the details a few minutes ago. It's kind of embarrassing, you know, for the top Earth diplomat on the station to be using a dating service. You'd think after fifteen years of practice negotiating with everything that walks, flies or crawls, I'd be a better judge of character. But somehow I always end up with the creeps, the basket cases, or the dreamers who can't stay around because they know that somewhere in space, there's a solid gold asteroid just waiting for them to stake a claim."

"And I'll bet that on every rock you've been posted, you left behind a broken hearted guy crying to his bar buddies that you loved your job more than him. You may be the top Earth representative within a hundred light years, but if you don't get moving, this career is going to be the only marriage you'll ever make."

"You sound like my mother," Kelly grumped, but she impulsively kissed her best friend on the cheek as she passed into the corridor. "Give my love to the girls."

"And you fill us in as soon as you get home. We want to know all the gory details. It's part of the deal," Donna warned her, before they headed off in separate directions. Donna's home was just a few minutes away on the same upscale residential deck as the consulate, while Kelly lived on a low-rent deck, populated mainly by station transients.

The corridors were lined with wall-height display panels that could show real-time feeds from exterior cameras or anything from station memory. At the moment, the displays were showing the riot of ships approaching and departing the station, and Kelly couldn't help but feel that familiar, yet transient thrill, that humans had finally reached the stars.

The fly in the ointment was that interstellar space travel had arrived for humanity through a remedial program run by a highly advanced race of artificial intelligences, the Stryx. Humans tended to think of the Stryx as robots, since some of them occupied mobile mechanical bodies to move about, but many lived in the structures of ships or space stations, and it was probable that others existed in forms that were beyond human comprehension.

Why they had assumed the role of nursemaids to the galaxy's low-achieving life forms was known as "The Mystery of the Stryx," and the robots weren't telling. The knowledge base of the Stryx was many orders of magnitude beyond that of the hundreds of life forms they nurtured, but it was suspected they were somewhat lacking in imagination, since they could find nothing better to do with their time than to interfere with the natural development of primitives. Biologicals who reached the stars under their own power often looked down their breathing protuberances at Earth and the other worlds the Stryx had taken under their metallic wings.

Kelly wasn't really interested in watching the comings and goings of starships tonight, even though her position as Earth's top diplomat on Union Station made her responsible for an endless parade of first contacts and requests for trade concessions. Well, perhaps that was a bit of an exaggeration, she confessed to herself, since interest in Earth was mainly limited to oxygen/nitrogen breathing aliens looking for cheap domestic help or a retro vacation experience. But in the two years since her arrival, Kelly had never regretted signing on to a five-year tour of duty on the farthest Stryx station from Earth, except for one little thing.

A chime sounded in her right ear, and ghostly letters spelling "Collect call from mother," suddenly appeared to be floating in space before her eyes. Kelly grimaced, turned into the primary radial corridor, then subvocalized, "Accept charges."

"I just had a terrible dream about you, Kelly." Her mother's voice sounded as clear as if she had been right there walking by Kelly's side. "You were thirty-five years old and you still weren't married, plus you moved all the way across the galaxy to a moon-sized alien space station where there weren't any eligible men."

"That's very funny, Mother," Kelly replied, rolling her eyes. "You know perfectly well that there are over four hundred thousand humans on Union Station these days, even if we're just a drop in the bucket of the total population. And how do you expect me to save enough money to buy my own apartment when each of these collect calls costs me a day's pay?"

"Oh, don't be such a killjoy," her mother chided. "I worry about you out there all alone while your younger brother and sister have settled down and started families. Besides, I don't call you that often."

"It's the third time this week, Mother!" Kelly suppressed a moan, forgetting that the subvoc pick-up embedded in her larynx would reproduce this as something like whoopee cushion sounds. Such minor foibles aside, the technology was so seamless that she had to study the lips of humanoids to figure out if they were speaking English, or if it was being simultaneously translated even as the sound from their native tongue was cancelled out by her ear implants.

"Have you been eating right, Kelly? I know you say that the restaurants synthesize the ingredients they can't import, but that doesn't mean the kitchen is kept clean."

"I can't talk now, Mother. I have a date," Kelly blundered, desperate to end the call.

"A date? You mean you're out on a date and you took a call from your mother? What's wrong with you?"

"I'm getting ready, Mom. I'm meeting him in an hour," Kelly answered, instantly regretting the explanation and rapping herself on the top of the head with her knuckles. Why hadn't she said, "You're right," and hung up? It was too late now.

"So who is he? How do you know him? Where are you meeting?"

"His name is Branch Miner, and we're meeting at a sports bar."

"Sounds romantic," her mother scoffed. "And how did you meet Mr. Miner?"

"I've got to go, Mom. There's somebody at the door." She didn't count it as a lie when her mother knew she was lying, which must have been the case since Kelly always used the same excuse to terminate a call. The excuse grew out of a rule of etiquette her mother had taught her about answering the phone while she was still living at home—never ignore a warm guest for a cold call.

"Don't be too picky, Kelly," her mother advised. "First impressions are often wrong. Why, your sister Lisa…"

"Bye, Mom," Kelly interrupted her mother and cut the connection. She fantasized briefly about paying a talent agency to find an out-of-work voice actress on Earth to take her mother's calls. Anything would be cheaper than the real-time tunneling communications billed triple for collect, and she was getting sore spots on her head from hitting herself in frustration. She took a left, narrowly escaped being run down by a bicycle messenger, and chose a rarely used stairwell door to descend three levels, bypassing the lift tubes.

Twenty-four months on Union Station and she had yet to go on a date worth a second look. Last week, to celebrate Kelly's two-year anniversary as Acting Consul, Donna had surprised her with a five-date subscription to the Eemas dating service. Eemas was rumored to be powered by the same Stryx that managed the station, which Kelly took as proof of how boring eternity must be for immortals. She had seen Eemas advertised and knew it must have cost Donna more than a week's pay, so the least Kelly could do was to show up for the dates. Besides, it turned out that Donna's pre-teen daughters were the driving force behind the gift for "poor Aunty Kelly," and that was a wake-up call to either find a man or get a new best friend.

Kelly exited the stairwell into the low-rent corridor that acted as the main artery of her neighborhood, and immediately slipped on a discarded pizza box, barely maintaining her balance. The omnipresent wall display panels were painted over with primitive murals depicting run-down inner-city scenes from Earth, images which were defaced in their turn by graffiti. The station maintenance bots came through and cleaned up on a regular schedule, but they didn't replace the display panels. The recently discarded trash, the loiterers and the transient homeless, made it clear that this wasn't anybody's dream neighborhood.

After a quick turn down a side corridor, Kelly arrived home in less than a hundred steps. The door to her cramped efficiency slid open in welcome, and she entered and collapsed with a groan into the LoveU massaging recliner which took up most of the floor space. The chair was her sole extravagance since arriving on Union Station, and she was still making ruinous payments on it. But the LoveU lived up to its name, offering an unconditional warm embrace with lower lumbar Shiatsu and gentle full-body kneading, alternating with low frequency vibration and Fintrian nerve stimulation of the arms, legs and neck.

"If you could walk and talk, you'd be the one I'd marry, LoveU," she murmured, stroking the armrests affectionately with her thumbs. The familiar chime sounded again in her ear, and "Libby" was suddenly floating before her eyes.

Kelly sighed and subvoced "Hi, Libby. Did you read my weekly? I'll bet you're the only one who does, and you don't even work for EarthCent."

"I always find your reports to be informative," replied the Stryx, who functioned as the station librarian and library, wrapped up in an extremely patient personality. After two years Kelly had come to suspect that Libby was one and the same as Gryph, the Stryx who ran the whole station, but if it preferred to manifest multiple personalities, that was none of her business.

"I also agree with your conclusion that Earth is fighting a losing battle trying to protect your limited exports," Libby continued. "Every planet goes through this stage. The best solution is to focus on your manufacturing strengths and to keep your prices reasonable, so that the counterfeiters will look elsewhere for easy money."

"I've been telling them that for years, but it doesn't seem to get through to the right people."

"An EarthCent representative's work is never done," Libby sympathized, or maybe it was a warning, Kelly could never be sure. "I forwarded a high-priority message for you earlier today and I hope you'll be able to act on it."

"Uh, I'm still working on that one, Libby. Is that why you called?"

"I just wanted to make sure you didn't fall asleep before your big date."

"You what? Are you the one running Eemas, along with whatever else you do?"

"Word gets around, Kelly. You know we Stryx aren't very good at keeping secrets," Libby replied innocently.

That's one clumsy evasion and one outright lie in a single statement, Kelly thought to herself. She suspected that Libby was employing some legal parsing that defined "very good" as "perfect." At least once a day, Kelly told herself that her ongoing confusion about the scope of her job duties was really due to some fundamental misapprehension on her own part. Everybody else seemed to accept the activities of the Stryx as a local force of nature, the space equivalent of weather, but Kelly was never sure whether it was sunny or raining.

She started to rise from the chair, and the LoveU instantly sensed her motion and practically rose on its hind legs to place her on her feet. Kelly once entertained the fantasy that when she died, rather than burial or cremation, she would be strapped into the chair and launched out into space to wander among the stars for eternity. But when she mentioned it to Donna, her friend had pointed out that she hadn't finished paying for the chair yet, and besides, it would be cruel to the LoveU. The latter part of the argument had convinced Kelly to abandon the idea.

"I'll leave you to get ready, then. We'll talk soon," Libby said through her implants, and withdrew. Kelly often wondered how many more of the hundred million plus sentient beings on the artificial world that was Union Station were speaking with the Stryx at the same instant. It was disconcerting to have a friend whose capabilities were unknown and probably unknowable for humans.

Kelly undressed quickly and punched up an express shower, which was as painful as it was invigorating. She imagined that the flagellants of Earth's history who scourged themselves with leather flails would have felt right at home in the shower, though they might have been upset over getting too wet, or even too clean for that matter. Ugh, why wouldn't her mind stop wandering? Maybe she'd ruined her brain by spending too much time reading.

When the water stopped, Kelly called for a pause to wrap her long red hair in a towel. Otherwise, the static electricity left over from the tornado drying sequence would turn her head into a giant red fuzz ball. She had learned that the hard way her second day on the station, when she walked out of the shower feeling ready to face the galaxy, looked in the mirror, and screamed. Come to think of it, that was how she originally made friends with Libby, who was always listening for anything out of the norm on the station.

Kelly rummaged through her one cramped closet and pulled out the black cocktail dress she always wore for diplomatic functions, an outfit Donna and the girls had locked her into by filling out all five of the Eemas encounter blanks in advance. The dating system was oddly inflexible. There were no videos or pictures, but Eemas was purported to have access to so much information that it knew people better than they knew themselves.

The application did give the subscriber an option to list any additional preferences, but Donna had wisely left those blank. Omniscience was the main point of the somewhat spooky ads for the service, and Kelly's date would just have to spot her based on, "long red hair, black dress, green eyes." The description Kelly received for Branch that afternoon was "tall, dark, beard," which is why she was intent on showing up early and letting him get stuck playing detective.

A half hour later, she finished with her hair and makeup, strapped on her black pumps, and headed out the door. One good thing about living on Union Station, or any place under the direct authority of the Stryx, was that a woman could walk the corridors of even the worst neighborhood in the dim night lighting, and not have to worry about anything worse than an unwanted business proposition.

Two

"Time," Kelly subvoced, and the Earth adjusted station time appeared in the corner of her eye. Great. Her first big date was already twenty minutes late. She gathered up the loose locks of silky red hair that had crept forward over her shoulders as she slouched at the bar and threw it all over her back. Then she made a conscious effort to sit up straight. "Like a lady," her mother would have said.

A few well-practiced eye movements triggered her holographic heads-up display to show the puzzling cable that Libby had forwarded from EarthCent after lunch. The content left her wondering if the diplomatic corps had started coding messages without supplying her with the key. That the budget conscious communications office insisted on the lowest cost tunneling telegraphic service didn't help either.

Belugian contract invalid stop must stop mining fleet stopping union station stop penalty clause stop operations stop authorized negotiations stop

Kelly sighed and took another sip of the ice water with a slice of lemon that the bartender had obligingly provided when she admitted to be waiting for a date. Earlier in the day, she had tried calling the diplomatic hotline for clarification, but either everybody had cleared out of EarthCent for the weekend or they were too broke to accept charges. EarthCent ran about nine hours ahead of the arbitrary station time the human residents had become accustomed to, so it really was Friday night on Earth.

The problem with working for Earth's Galactic Diplomatic Center was that it represented Earth without any cooperation or budgetary assistance from the endlessly bickering national governments, the existence of which the Stryx barely acknowledged and clearly didn't take seriously. EarthCent was basically imposed on the planet in a take-it-or-leave-it arrangement, a standard procedure the intelligent robots had evolved through hundreds of first contacts.

True, the Stryx recruited humans for all of the jobs at EarthCent, through a mysterious process that eliminated the need to apply for a position. Like Kelly, potential EarthCent employees were simply contacted out of the blue and offered a job. Everybody from the lowest paid spaceport courtesy shuttle driver to the top cluster ambassador was handpicked.

But other than the occasional indecipherable communication, EarthCent offered no guidance for employees in the field. It was more like an employment agency for an independent diplomatic service. In the course of the last fifteen years, Kelly had received the drunken confidences of many an EarthCent diplomat at various embassy and consular functions. The only explicit instruction any of them had received from EarthCent was in the initiation oath, to do their best for humanity.

Two years into her tour as Earth's top diplomat on the most important space station in the sector, Kelly still wasn't sure about the boundaries of her job. When aliens contacted her office looking for information about Earth, she tried to answer their questions and generally point them in the right direction. When invitations to diplomatic events arrived, she dutifully strapped on her high heels, slipped on her black dress, and checked with Libby to make sure that the atmosphere at the party wouldn't dissolve her lungs or melt her skin.

Kelly used to believe she was going through an extended trial period, after which EarthCent or the Stryx would cue her in on the big picture. Recently, she was beginning to suspect there was no overarching strategy. Instead, Gryph often questioned her about the misbehavior of humans on the regional galactic scene, and more than once she found that her responses had been acted on as if she had the final say in all things human related. It was definitely a little humbling, and when people asked her what she did for work, she had to restrain herself from answering, "I'm sort of responsible for humanity within a hundred light years." The consul's job apparently encompassed the judicial, executive and legislative branches all in one, and her salary didn't quite cover her living expenses.

authorized negotiations stop

Did that mean she was authorized to negotiate with these Belugians she'd never heard of before today, or was the message referring to some third party? All she'd been able to find out was that "Belugians" referred to a chartered mutual company that included members from various species. How was she to locate the contract holders, much less negotiate, when she didn't know what they wanted or what she could offer? Kelly's thoughts were interrupted, and she jumped in her chair as a hot hand clasped her bare shoulder and spun her stool away from the bar.

"Long red hair, black dress, green eyes," a raspy baritone pronounced. "Barkeep, I'll have what she's having."

Kelly fought back the urge to stand up and leave. She hated when strange men put their hands on her without so much as a how-do-you-do, but she had promised Donna and the girls to spend at least a half hour with each date to give the man a chance. The service was so expensive that she intended to think of the dates as the best paying work she would ever have in her life. Instead of stalking out or throwing her ice water in his face, she reached up and removed his hand from her bare shoulder, returning it to him with a tight smile.

"I'm Kelly. You must be Branch," she said, trying not to sound downright hostile as she surveyed his tall, dark, bearded form. Not unhandsome, she decided, in a piratical sort of way. But way too aggressive and overconfident, and probably one of those guys who figures conversation is a waste of time.

"Branch I am," he replied, taking her first salvo in stride and settling onto the stool next to her. "Is this your first Eemas hook-up?"

"Actually, it is." She regarded him quizzically, pondering his choice of words. "Did I do something to give it away?"

"Oh, no," he laughed. "I just wondered, since it's the first time I've done anything like this. Never needed help meeting ladies," he concluded with a wink and a friendly leer.

"So what possessed you to shell out for tonight?" she inquired wryly.

"Shell out?" Branch appeared puzzled for a moment, and he ran his eyes over her exposed skin, as if looking for seams. "Oh, you mean pay. No, I didn't pay. I just got an invitation from this Eemas thing when we docked a few hours ago. I was going to visit a hostess house with the rest of the crew. It's kind of a tradition with sailors, you know. But when I saw your picture, I had to come."

"Picture? You got a picture?" Kelly almost squeaked in aggravation. "And you didn't have to pay?"

"Easy, Red. I just said that, didn't I?" Branch took the ice water the bartender brought him and drained it in one gulp. An expression that combined amusement with distaste fled across his features, and he shook his head in mock despair as he returned the empty glass to the bar. "You really do know how to party, don't you?" he commented, and then continued without giving her a chance to respond. "So, shall we go back to your quarters, or would you rather we rent a room? I'm feeling generous so it's my treat."

"What? Wait!" Kelly sputtered, after Branch rose and started for the exit as if her only logical option was to follow after him like a lost puppy. "What do you think this is? I mean, I came for a date!"

"A date?" Branch hesitated and stepped back to the bar. He fingered the wedge of lemon on his empty water glass and took a long look at the tray of sliced fruit on the bartending station. Then he shook his head and said, "Oh, a date! I can do that, sure. Would a half hour be enough?"

"A half hour would be perfect," Kelly answered with a cold smile, and brought up a digital stopwatch display in the corner of her eye. Then she had a pleasant thought and advanced the countdown from thirty minutes to twenty-six, to account for her last four minutes on dating duty.

"Well, would you like something to eat, or should we just get some real drinks and talk?" Branch asked, settling back onto his stool with the ease of a veteran campaigner.

"Talking could be nice," Kelly replied, swirling the ice in her glass for the reassuring tinkling sound it made. "You mentioned you just got in, so what brings you to Union Station?"

"Union has the best cross-galactic tunnel rates on this side of the lens," he quoted from the repeating welcome message that greeted all approaching ships, at the same time signaling to the bartender. "And if you can keep a secret, we're picking up some obsolete disintegrator projectors, good war surplus stuff left over from the Yeridum/Mudirey conflict."

"I've never heard of either—wait, that sounded like the same name spelled backwards," Kelly ventured. She had always been proud of her aptitude for pattern recognition and ability with numbers, and she secretly believed that these were the talents for which the Stryx had plucked her out of obscurity halfway through her sophomore year in university. After a brief EarthCent training course, she had been set on the bottom rung of the diplomatic ladder, which she had been steadily climbing ever since.

The arrival of the bartender offered a break in the flow of the conversation, and Kelly ordered a screwdriver, while Branch asked for a Divverflip. "One screwdriver and one Drazen Divverflip, coming up." After repeating the order, the bartender favored Kelly with a curious look of appraisal, and then retreated towards the collection of bottles at the center of the long bar.

"Of course, that's why it's also called the Mirror War." Branch continued their conversation with just the slightest hint of condescension, not unusual from a man discovering that a woman lacks his enthusiasm for archaic conflicts. "The Yeridum accidentally broke into a parallel universe—but you aren't really interested in all that." He cut himself off to Kelly's surprise, just as her features were beginning to go slack. Maybe he wasn't that insensitive after all, she thought, or maybe he's just that desperate.

"Are you some kind of pirate that you're in the market for disintegrator weapons?" Kelly joked, or at least she hoped it was a joke.

"Not these days," Branch replied. He rubbed the side of his nose significantly, and glanced around the lounge to see if anybody was obviously eavesdropping on their conversation. Kelly knew that there was no true privacy on the station, because the Stryx had built the place, and probably kept every molecule under surveillance. But the robots were also famous for minding their own business and letting the biologicals have at it, as long as they followed the local rules.

"Disintegrator projectors were lousy weapons, since they work so slowly and most targets aren't going to stay still long enough for them to do much damage," he continued. "But they're useful for peeling surface layers off a planet from space if you have enough power. A great tool for terraforming and such."

The bartender returned with Kelly's screwdriver and a smoking purple concoction which looked like toxic waste that had been remediated with food dye. Kelly took a sip of her screwdriver, which was excellent, and received a wink from the bartender, who waited around to watch Branch sample his Divverflip. Branch tipped the glass up for a taste, and then drained half the contents at a go. The two males exchanged approving head nods, and then the bartender moved off to greet new patrons.

"I've always been interested in terraforming," Kelly fibbed. She relaxed into bad date mode, hoping that remaking planets was a subject that could get them painlessly through the remaining twenty something minutes. Besides, she found it paid to keep her ears open, as Libby was fond of hinting that human knowledge was limited more by laziness than by storage capacity. "Is that what you do?"

Branch considered the question and scratched absently behind his ear. "Well, it's not really terraforming if you stop halfway through, more like strip mining. But what's wrong now?" he demanded in annoyance, seeing that Kelly had turned white and was staring behind his head.

"What was THAT?" she asked in a hollow voice, as a feeling of dread climbed up her chest.

"What was what?" Branch sounded honestly perplexed, and swiveled his stool around to see if he was missing something behind him.

"That!" she cried, pointing at the movement under his jacket between the shoulder blades. "You have a tentacle! I saw you scratch your ear with it!"

Now Branch started to look angry. "Of course I have a tentacle, what kind of Drazen do you take me for? I'm beginning to see why this stupid hook-up service is free."

"It's not free, it's expensive," Kelly exploded. "And it set me up with an alien!"

"What are you, some kind of xenophobe?" Branch asked incredulously, as if interspecies dating was the norm throughout the civilized galaxy.

"Xenophobe? Take that back," Kelly hissed, her green eyes sparking anger of her own. "I'm Earth's diplomatic liaison to Union Station, and I've been working with aliens for—"

"Oh, so everybody who isn't from your precious Earth is an alien," Branch interrupted her, and then he stopped and stared at nothing for a moment, as if he was reading from a heads-up holographic display of his own. "Uh, did you say, Earth?"

"Yes, I said Earth. What, are you getting your lame pick-up lines from a teleprompter? Wait, you don't even speak English, do you? I knew there was something funny about you, but all that facial hair makes it hard to see your lips..." Kelly trailed off, blushing and biting her tongue to keep from blaming her mistake on the lighting in the bar being poor, or her eyes being tired from overwork.

"English? Why would I speak an archaic language from a strip mining claim?" Branch's expression showed his frustration at the turn in the conversation. "And why would a world with diplomatic representation on Union Station bargain away mining rights to an entire continent in return for some old Drazen jump ships?"

"A continent?" Kelly's jaw dropped. "Wait, you work for Belugian?"

"Stakeholder, second class." Branch drew himself up and looked like he was waiting for a compliment. Kelly's mind raced as she stalled for time, pouring out every bit of a "My, aren't you a handsome alien," vibe she could muster. Negotiations authorized, she said to herself.

"Branch," Kelly said, swinging her chair toward him. Crossing her legs and repressing a shudder, she put her hand on his forearm. "Could I tell you a diplomatic secret without it getting back to Earth where you heard it?"

A strange but not unpleasant odor filled the air, probably the Drazen way of saying she had his full attention. He looked at her expectantly.

"I shouldn't be interfering in commercial dealings, of course, but I happen to know that the Belugian contract is invalid," she cooed, smiling and batting her eyes for good measure.

Branch's own eyes hardened like olive pits as he swiveled his seat back towards the bar, drained the rest of his Divverflip, and signaled for another. Apparently the schoolgirl approach wasn't going to buy her anything, but the refill meant he wasn't planning on getting up and leaving.

"My information shows that the contract was signed and bonded in the presence of a Thark recorder. There can be no question of validity," he added evenly, all of the friendliness gone from his voice.

"I'm well aware of the Thark role in commercial law," Kelly replied with a light laugh, again playing for time as she hurriedly queried Libby for information on Thark recorders. No loopholes there, she'd have to try a shot in the dark. "But what would you say if I told you the party who signed for Earth lacked legal standing?"

Branch's tentacle reappeared to scratch absently in his thick hair, and he toyed with his toxic drink and stared at nothing while exercising his own information implants. Then he turned towards her and said, "Are you going to pretend that the Elected Government of North America isn't authorized to treat for mineral rights?"

"The Elected Government of North America?" She almost giggled in relief. "That's a student group. I was in the Senate before my braces were off. It's just school kids playing at running things," she concluded, and offered Branch a sympathetic smile.

Branch's eyes unfocused and he tilted his head to one side, leading Kelly to assume he was now conferencing with his colleagues or management. She made use of the time to take a long sip from her screwdriver and to ask Libby to dig through any relevant Earth news about the student government, just to make sure they hadn't staged a coup in recent years and taken over North America for real. The truth was, the Stryx weren't the only ones who didn't take the national governments very seriously anymore.

Back before the Stryx opened Earth, they flooded the existing communications networks with information about the galaxy, bypassing the governmental monopoly on information. After the preparatory period, they delivered advanced technology and off-world transportation on credit, so interstellar trading and human labor exchanges had taken off. Other than collecting taxes when their former citizens were dumb enough to use the banking infrastructure, there just wasn't much the old governments could do about it.

Whoops, there it was. Libby had found the contract with the Belugians in a student paper under the headline, "Returning Seniors Trade Rocks Rights for Jump Ships." Damn, the contract language looked pretty serious, and the signees were the elected representatives of over thirty million school kids in a galaxy where some species took the rights of children seriously.

"The penalty clause gives your people the choice of cancelling the contract by paying with labor levies or Yttrium," Branch reported after a long pause. "That's ten thousand labor years or ten thousand kilograms of

Yttrium. If you can provide me with the delivery details, I'm authorized to arrange for the pick-up."

"Oh, I don't think that will be necessary," Kelly answered in her best diplomatic tone. "After all, you must acknowledge that these kids weren't authorized to negotiate for anybody other than themselves."

"So they'll be supplying the labor levies," Branch continued without missing a beat. "We'd prefer to take the older students, of course, but the younger children could be useful for working in low tunnels underground, not to mention cleaning those hard to reach places between the gears in the mining equipment."

Kelly furiously skimmed the fine print on her heads-up display, looking for a way to avoid a diplomatic incident without sending ten thousand North American children into virtual slavery for a year. Then she spotted the clause for computing the length of servitude that left the distribution of time over laborers to be determined by the humans. A little quick math and she had her solution.

"Well, I'm not sure how transporting ten million children off Earth for around eight hours is going to make any profit for Belugian, especially after you knock off the time they spend waiting in line to board. But if you insist on enforcing the penalty clause, I suppose their parents will enjoy the free babysitting."

Branch slammed his drink down on the bar and his tentacle stood out rigidly above his head. Kelly realized that she was looking at one angry Drazen.

"So this is how humans keep their contracts," he exploded. "You know perfectly well that ten thousand labor years should be in standard ten year commitments. A thousand workers for ten years."

22

"I know nothing of the sort, Branch." Kelly smiled widely and gave a little laugh. "Just as you apparently haven't heard that on Earth, children have no legal standing to bind themselves by contract."

"Primitive backwater," he snorted, his tentacle wilting over his shoulder. Branch fiddled with his glass, stared off into nothingness for a bit, then grunted. "Look, the truth is that this came to us through some planet chaser working on spec for a finder's fee. But a deal's a deal, don't you agree? We've already committed to buy four disintegrator projectors for the job, and they just aren't much use for anything else. My people think the penalty clause will stand up in Thark Chancery, even if it gets cut back to actual damages. Of course, the litigation will go on for years if you fight, and that will come to much more than the projectors are worth, but there's a principle at stake here for Belugian. We can't just start waiving contracts for whoever suffers sellers regret or we'd be out of business, if not at war."

Kelly hesitated. She didn't really know if her consulate had a budget for anything beyond keeping the office open. When the need arose she gave stranded humans small handouts out of her own pocket, or raided the petty cash that the consulate generated from the service fees charged to aliens who refused to believe in something for nothing. Neither EarthCent nor Gryph had ever offered a clear answer to her questions about budgeting, they shared a genius for politely changing the subject, but she suspected there were going to be costs involved this time no matter what she decided.

"Alright, here's what we can do for you." Kelly tried to sound as reluctant as possible while pretending to be in silent conversation with her non-existent superiors. "Send my consulate the contact information for your disintegrator supplier, and my people will negotiate a penalty for cancelling the order. If the supplier insists on delivery, we'll take two projectors, but you'll have to take the other two. Do we have a deal?"

Branch looked relieved and extended his hand, fingers up, like he was pushing on an invisible wall. "Deal," he said, and after a brief moment of confusion, Kelly extended her hand to meet his, noticing for the first time that he had an extra thumb.

"Well that was an interesting half hour," Branch continued, reverting to his earlier form. "Are you ready to join me for a little celebration now?"

"I never mix business with pleasure," Kelly replied, attempting to sound regretful for the sake of the Drazen's ego. Branch made a show of searching his clothing for something and then claimed to have forgotten his money pouch on the ship. Kelly just smiled and shooed him away, relieved to have solved the Belugian contract emergency for the cost of a couple drinks. She was sure he'd find his money easily enough when he caught up with his crew.

Three

When Joe McAllister heard that the disintegrator sale was off the table, he breathed a deep sigh of relief. He'd been sweating over how to get the antique weapons hot for a demo, but he couldn't draw sufficient power from station distribution, probably a good thing for the structural integrity of the hold.

Joe had even considered offering the weapons to the buyer for scrap weight just to free up precious space in Mac's Bones, the junkyard he'd won in a card game three years earlier while waiting for a new deployment. It had been a struggle ever since to pay the rent on the hold stuffed full of random alien spacefaring artifacts, the nameplates of which could have served as the galaxy's Rosetta Stone for "No user serviceable parts."

That morning, an EarthCent apparatchik had contacted Mac's Bones out of the blue and offered to pay a cancellation fee on the disintegrator deal. After some minor blustering in an attempt to get the price up, he'd settled for twenty-five hundred Stryx creds, which would pay the rent for another cycle. Consequently, Joe was in a good mood as he showered and dressed for his first introduction through the Eemas service.

After years of being inundated with Eemas ads through every form of station media, he had to admit he was curious to find out if the service was as good as its frightening reputation. Frightening for a forty-year-old bachelor. Thanks to a barter deal for a salvaged Alterian fuel pack with less than a quarter of its power remaining, Joe was the proud owner of a second-hand Eemas subscription with just one date used.

The original owner had been so desperate to fire up his little scout ship and get off the station that he threw in his silver suit of clothes to sweeten the deal. Unfortunately, the guy had sported a lower center of gravity than Joe's rangy frame, so the sleeves were a bit short and the cut was somewhat baggy. But Union Station fashions were eclectic, to say the least, and Joe believed that even his grandfather's beekeeper gear would have gone unremarked at a party.

Paul tilted up his chin and squinted against the reflections coming off the suit when Joe finished dressing, but he didn't say anything, which was normal for the thirteen year old. Paul had been a sort of mascot for Joe's squad since the age of eight, when they had pulled the starving boy from the wreckage of a smelter on a mining colony that had been raided and destroyed. The raiders were long gone by the time Joe's squad arrived, and the constant sandstorms had already buried any bodies left on the surface, so they never found out if Paul's parents were dead or taken captive.

When Joe won Mac's Bones in the card game, he decided to leave the mercenaries and try running the business himself, partly to give Paul a home where the kid could meet some other children. That and the fact that as Joe aged, the mercenary retirement plan of dying with your boots on had been sounding less and less attractive.

"You go to bed. I may be back late," he instructed Paul, before exiting their spacious if crude quarters in the crew module of a scrapped ice harvester which had lost a fight with a comet's tail. The remains of the vessel sat in an improvised cradle near the entrance of the hold that contained Mac's Bones. As part of the inner docking and warehousing deck, the space featured the highest ceilings on the station, but the floor curvature was more noticeable than on the outer decks.

Some show-off civilizations employed artificial black holes at the center of spherical space stations to create gravitational pull, but they were a technical nightmare to build and maintain, and ridiculously expensive in fuel for arriving and departing ships. The space stations built by the Stryx were all versions of an enormous, slowly spinning cylinder, with a vast hollow core to accommodate shipping traffic, and hundreds of concentric decks to satisfy the gravitational preferences of biological tenants.

The atmospheric plugs in Joe's nose hummed happily, as if they enjoyed the challenge of filtering breathable air out of the witch's brew of gases that filled the shared areas of the station, such as the lift tube from the docking deck to the residential areas. Many of the humans who frequented mixed sections of the station wore the plugs in a little locket around their necks, so that they were always available when needed.

It took tourists a while to get accustomed to the plugs, and humans had to remember not to breathe through their mouths, but versions of the same technology allowed many species to mingle in shared areas of the space station. The simple plugs worked in sections where the atmosphere contained enough oxygen and nitrogen for them to filter, but if the ratio of the gases was too far off, they would start to overheat, a phenomenon known as "nose burn."

After less than a minute in transit, the capsule finished its run and came to a halt at Joe's destination on the upscale human recreational and residential deck. He emerged and took a few cautious steps to adjust to the minor increase in gravity, feeling all the while like a tourist in his flashy suit.

The Eemas date was scheduled for 20:30 hours in Chinatown, which meant he had some time to kill if he was going to arrive fashionably late. No points scored by looking needy, he told himself. Instead, he strolled in the opposite direction towards the Little Apple, a sort of melting pot of Earth cultures, though few of the activities that took place in the Little Apple could be described as cultural events.

Joe ducked reflexively at the sound of popping champagne corks as he strode past the Elvis chapel, where a lucky couple of somethings with two legs and one head each had just tied the knot. Champagne corks popping reminded him of the sound of the goo throwers his men had come up against in the Bereftian action. The goo stuck to armor and deployed an army of nanobots, turning the casualty into—ugh, he'd rather not think about it.

"Flowers for your lady, sir?" piped up a small girl, tugging at his suit sleeve. She was ten or twelve, with a basket of what appeared to be fresh-cut roses on her arm. The girl was small for her age, and somebody had applied fake smudges of grime to her face, as if there was some secret slum where the station's maintenance bots would allow dirt to accumulate. It came to him that he'd never been accosted by a flower girl before, which he took as a vote of confidence in the silver suit.

"Uh, I can take one, I guess," Joe replied awkwardly. Although he'd been conducting a largely one-sided conversation with Paul for five years, Joe wasn't very good at talking with children, especially little girls.

"The ladies usually expect a dozen," the girl pushed her pitch with wide-eyed sincerity. "It's 5 centees for one or 20 for a dozen, so it's almost like I'm robbing you if you don't take twelve."

"Oh, alright then, a dozen," he agreed, making a mental note to cross to the other side of the pedestrian corridor the next time he saw a flower girl waiting. She expertly counted out a dozen roses and wrapped a bit of sticky foil around the stems to keep them together. Joe dug through his pockets and extracted a 25-centee piece for the girl.

Small trade in the station economy was carried out with Stryx creds and a few other hard currencies from the local empires, bypassing the tyranny of electronic money. Only for the largest transactions did anybody resort to financial intermediaries, and the more trustworthy species managed to avoid banks completely through a combination of barter and promissory notes.

"Here you are, sir. Mind the thorns," the girl cautioned, as she handed him the roses and took the coin. "Will you be needing change, sir?"

"Uh, I guess not," Joe mumbled, and quickly moved away from the petite mugger. Maybe electronic money had some advantages after all, but most of the galaxy's denizens preferred hard cash for privacy reasons. Earth was the only planet he knew where people paid for items with their bulky communication devices, something that had slowed the adoption of the subvoc and translation implants that were otherwise omnipresent throughout civilized space. But he hadn't been back to Earth in the twenty years since his parents were killed in a car accident and he shipped out as a mercenary, so maybe things had changed.

The aroma from varied ingredients sizzling in hot woks filled the air as Joe reached Chinatown and headed to the Great Panda Pagoda, where the date was scheduled. He was looking for a woman with very long black hair and black fingernails with gold stripes. Since he hadn't gotten around to checking with Eemas about the process for resetting the subscription, Joe was curious to see what kind of woman the service had picked out for the former owner of the suit.

Wading through the tightly packed tables, Joe focused on the gold-striped fingernails angle, as many of the female patrons favored long black hair. Finally he spotted a tall, imperious looking woman with an elaborate ponytail as long as his arm and a sleeveless top made out of gold metallic mesh that extended right up her neck to the underside of her jaw. She was standing in the entrance of a private cubby off to one side of the service counter, and after making eye contact, she entered it without waiting for him to approach. For some odd reason, his brief glimpse of the gold stripes on her long black fingernails reminded him of the warning coloration sported by some poisonous creatures on Earth.

"Hi, I'm Joe," he said, mustering his best smile as he entered the private cubby. "Sorry if I'm a bit late. I got held up in the Little Apple."

His date fixed him with a cold glare as he pulled out a chair and sat down across from her at the tiny round table. This isn't going well at all, he thought to himself, and added, "I brought you these," extending the bouquet as a peace offering.

"How sweet of you," she purred, taking the flowers. "I am the Lady Talia." As soon as she found her grip on the foil wrapped around the stems, she leaned across the table and lightly slapped him across the face with the blooms. The rose petals mainly held together, though he got one stuck in his teeth, which might teach him not to open his mouth in surprise.

"What the hell!" Joe exploded.

"I don't like it when a man isn't on time, Joe," she answered, pronouncing his name with undisguised disdain, as if it didn't come up to her standard of sophistication.

"I said I was sorry. I hope you don't let this spoil the evening," he replied after a short staring contest, during which he didn't like what he saw. "Why don't we order something? I know I'd feel better with some food in my stomach."

"I ordered for us already, Joe. I'm sure that was your intention in any case," she added with a cold little chuckle.

"Am I missing something here?" Joe asked, not sure if he was more annoyed with Lady Talia, the Eemas service, or the former owner of the subscription, who he was beginning to realize may have had some quirks.

"Let's get right to the point, Joe. You tell me why I should accept a badly dressed man who doesn't arrive on time into my harem." She drummed the long black nails of her free hand on the tabletop. "I'm waiting."

"Look, you've got this all wrong," Joe protested. "You see, I got this suit and the dating subscription in a trade with a guy for a fuel pack, and I didn't get around to informing Eemas of the change." Then he laughed and broke into the wide, open smile that had cracked the defenses of more than one woman in the old days. "It's kind of funny when you think about it. I mean, we'll both have a good story."

"Joe, Joe, Joe," she drawled slowly, as if she was trying to provoke him. "You don't expect me to believe that hogwash. I could see from the moment you entered the restaurant that you crave a strong hand on the reins. I could see it in the way you crossed the floor and how you squirm about on your seat like you're afraid somebody will touch you. And I will touch you, Joe, but only when I choose to do so."

"Now, just set that shuttle down, lady, I mean, Lady Talia. I don't like sitting with my back to a roomful of people, that's just common sense, and I can order my own damn food if it's all the same to you."

"You're fighting me, Joe," she reprimanded him, but the corners of her mouth turned up and her eyes began to sparkle. "I like a man who knows how to play this game."

Joe stood up and shoved his chair back from the table. "I'm getting the hell out of here, lady. I'm sorry I screwed up your evening. Better luck next time." He pulled aside the curtain and walked out of the booth.

"Joe," she called after him mockingly. "Eemas knows you better than you know yourself. You'll never find happiness unless you accept that."

He flipped a hand at her dismissively without turning around as he worked his way through the clustered tables towards the exit.

"Joe!" He could hear her laughter as the restaurant fell quiet in enjoyment of the free entertainment. "You'll be back."

It's not just me who won't be back, he mused, as he headed towards the Little Apple for a burger. Now I know why the former owner of this suit was in such a hurry to get off the station. I've got to contact Eemas tomorrow and find out about updating that subscription.

But as he sat watching the people strolling by the Burger Bar, nursing his beer and wiping up stray smears of ketchup with the few remaining fries, he found himself wondering what kind of woman the omniscient Eemas would spring on him for real. All of a sudden, it was kind of scary, just like the ads.

Four

"Congratulations, Kelly." Stanley welcomed her with a hearty handshake as he let her into the condo he shared with Donna and their girls. "From acting consul to full consul in two years. That must be some kind of record."

Kelly couldn't figure out if this was intended as a compliment or a consolation, since she didn't know how long it usually took to make full consul, but she knew Stanley meant well in either case.

"Thank you, Stan." Kelly dipped her head in acknowledgement and followed him into the kitchen, where Donna was working on some complicated dessert.

The ambient apartment lighting was much brighter than the hall outside, about as bright as early afternoon on Earth, so she assumed the girls had talked their parents into a modified schedule. Blythe and Chastity were engaged in artistically smearing something that looked like burnt molasses onto each other's faces, which struck Kelly as a little immature for girls their age.

"Grab a seat, Kelly. I'll just be another minute. If I don't mix in the Thorian spice-starch at the precise temperature and time, the tarts could burst into flames," Donna explained, and then paused to think. "Or maybe they'll turn green, which would be even worse."

"No hurry. I've got a half hour before my date," Kelly replied. "So what are my silly girls up to?"

"We're not silly!" the girls replied in chorus, followed by gales of laughter and the impromptu chant, "You'll never guess, you'll never guess."

"Are you fighting?" Kelly asked, always a good first guess when engaged in a game of twenty questions with children on the station.

"No," the girls squealed, wiping their hands on dresses that looked like something from a history book, which drew Kelly's attention to the fact that they weren't wearing their typical one-piece jumpsuits.

"What's going on?" Kelly directed her question to Donna since Stan had already retreated to his sports room. Despite his expertise as a knowledge trader for a gaming guild, Stan was always the softest touch for family information since he was oblivious to the value of secrets that didn't advance game play.

"Have you seen the immersive release of 'My Fair Lady' yet?" Donna answered her question with a question, a habit that drove Kelly nuts at work almost every day. Guessing games and making up stories were extremely popular with the children on the station, much more so than she remembered from her own youth. The problem was that it seemed to rub off on their parents, so Kelly found it difficult to get a straight answer from anybody who had kids at home.

"You know I avoid the immersives," she replied. "Smelling and tasting things that aren't there, feeling weather that isn't real, giving the projectors direct access to my implants. The whole thing is too creepy, and it just makes me dizzy."

"Poor Aunty Kelly," said Blythe, and the twelve year old shook her head in mock despair. "I guess you're never going find out our secret."

"I think I remember the story," Kelly said hopefully. "A lower class woman learns how to speak nicely in exchange for chocolate. Right?"

Donna slid the tray of tarts into the oven and told it "Thorian spice tarts." The oven thought it over for a microsecond before loading the proper program and displaying a countdown to completion.

"The lower-class woman was Eliza Doolittle, and she was a poor flower girl," Donna explained. She pulled out a chair and sat down across from Kelly. "My daughters liked the idea of being poor flower girls so much that they convinced one of the nursery owners from an ag deck to let them try selling flowers on consignment around the cafes in the evening."

"Except we aren't poor," Chastity said, holding out a handful of change. "Look!"

"We made more in two nights than you pay mommy for a whole week," Blythe added, half accusing, half proud.

"You know that your mom doesn't really work for me," Kelly defended herself. "We both work for EarthCent, which really means the Stryx, and your mother is actually the one whose job it is to pay me!"

"Oh, speaking of which, you got a raise to go with your new title," Donna told her brightly.

"They didn't tell me," Kelly said excitedly. She held up her hands with fingers crossed. "How much can I expect next payday? I'm behind on the rent again, and the smart aleck landlord program has been fooling with the water temperature when I take a shower. It's just a matter of time before it starts in with varying the room temperature and piping in nasty odors."

"Ah, I think it will come to a hundred and twenty creds," Donna replied, sounding a little embarrassed.

"But that's less than I'm making now!" Kelly wailed, causing the girls to stop what they were doing and look on in interest. "It's less than you make. It's less than the poor flower girls are making!"

"It will go up again eventually, but there was a garnishment order from EarthCent. Something about paying a contract cancellation fee to a junkyard called Mac's Bones?"

"Oh, no," Kelly groused. "I thought I was authorized to negotiate a settlement. I guess the EarthCent version of negotiation doesn't include hard cash."

"Anyway, I put you on a payment plan so you'll still have some walking around money," Donna added sympathetically. "Otherwise, you would have had no income for ten months."

"Barter is better," piped up a begrimed Chastity, echoing one of the cheery mantras of the Stryx school system, which offered a full range of educational opportunities to anybody who was willing to work in exchange. The labor that the Stryx demanded from young children involved playing with small robots for a couple of hours a day, but the children all seemed to take their duties seriously.

"We could give you a loan, Aunty Kelly," Blythe offered. When she saw the crestfallen expression on Kelly's face, she added generously, "You don't really have to pay it back."

"You're just making it worse," Donna chided the girls gently. "Aunty Kelly has a very important job, and someday she'll make a living at it. Now run along to work or you'll miss the dinner rush." The girls immediately recovered their high spirits and flounced out of the apartment trading lines in imagined cockney accents.

"Don't look so glum, Kelly," Donna continued. "You know the last thing the girls would want is for you to feel bad about earning less in a week than they make in a few hours on the weekend." Kelly buried her face in her arms, and Donna had to add, "Oh, I didn't mean it that way either. You're really getting too sensitive lately. What do you know about tonight's date?"

"I know it has to be better than last week's," Kelly responded, perking up. "At least, it can't turn out as expensive, can it?"

"Well, the Stryx have an odd way of running a dating service, that's for sure. But I'll bet the children who grew up here would take it all in stride. I guess it's their education system, but it's too late for us, of course," Donna concluded with a smile.

"I love my job, there's nothing I'd rather be doing. I just wish I could get Libby or EarthCent to give me a little more guidance," Kelly grumbled. "I mean, I'm happy they upgraded my status to full consul, at least I won't have to keep explaining to aliens that 'acting consul' didn't mean I was pretending. You'd think somebody would have fixed the translation algorithms by this time."

"You're married to the job, and that's your problem. You care more about getting in the middle of every crisis that comes up than you do about finding a man. I think you're actually embarrassed by the fact that the humans who come out here act just as badly as they did on Earth."

"I'm the one who gets stuck explaining it all to Gryph," Kelly argued. "And I'm taking this dating business very seriously. Did I tell you I'm meeting him in the excursion ship section and we're taking a core and cylinder tour? I've never been."

"Stan took me for an anniversary date a couple of years ago. It would have been very romantic except the weightlessness made us both queasy. Then the excursion craft looped against the station rotation and all of that spinning made me throw up. Stan saw it coming and caught it all in his cap before it reached the bulkhead, and later I found out that he bribed the tour operator to give him the video of it from the cabin camera. Hey, do you want to watch it?" Donna asked.

"Thank you for the lovely memory and for offering me an instant replay of you sicking up just before I board," Kelly replied sarcastically. "I think I'll take a pass on coffee and dessert now."

"I'm sorry," Donna apologized. "I guess I wasn't thinking. But you have yourself a good time, and remember that behind every unopened door lurks a monster."

"What does that even mean?" Kelly asked, but then she decided not to give Donna a chance for an explanation that could ruin the date before it began. "Never mind. I'll ask Libby about it if I'm too early. See you at the office."

"I expect you to let me know how it went the minute you get home," Donna reminded Kelly, as she followed her to the door. "I'll be up late helping the girls count their change in any case."

Donna's comment reminded Kelly of something that had been bothering her since she entered the apartment, so she stopped just short of the proximity field that activated the door. "I noticed when I came in that your apartment lighting seems to be on a different schedule than the corridor areas on this deck. Don't you worry about the girls being tired for school?"

"You're still thinking in Earth terms, with all those school buses and early schedules that had nothing to do with what suited the children's natural rhythms. Here, the kids follow their own schedule, since it makes no difference to the Stryx when children want their lessons or put in their service time. If you want to scare the station kids into behaving, just hint that they might be happier back on Earth or some other planet."

"Funny, I never really noticed," Kelly admitted. "I guess it's because my previous postings were on planets. This is my first extended stay on a station. Thanks, and wish me luck."

"Luck," Donna offered enthusiastically as the door slid closed.

Kelly slowly worked her way down towards the excursion dock, thinking about her own childhood on Earth. Billions of people had voted with their feet before Kelly was born, making humans the latest wave of colonists and cheap labor migrants to compatible worlds circling thousands of stars. Wherever the Stryx had influence, intelligent robots enjoyed the same legal status as biologicals. So human labor only had to compete with non-thinking robots, and those "mechanicals" weren't flexible enough to do many jobs. Intelligent robots had few needs and could always find better work than harvesting crops and doing manual labor, not to mention a strong preference for the clean environment of outer space.

The excursion bay on the inner docking deck featured slightly lower apparent gravity than Kelly was used to, so she had to walk gingerly to avoid bouncing off her high heels. Any other time she would have worn deck shoes with their magnetic sticky cleats, but the black pumps practically belonged to the cocktail dress. She was on the lookout for "black suit, black tie, black hat," which made her date sound like he was either a country western singer or an undertaker.

Kelly's date had arrived before her, and was fidgeting about nervously next to the gangway of an expensive looking cabin cruiser, which made her feel a little better after Donna's uninspiring tourism tale. The ship appeared much more spaceworthy than she had expected for an excursion craft, and she was also glad that she wasn't the only one who looked a little nervous.

"Welcome, welcome. I'm Olaf Thorgudson." He greeted Kelly energetically and he extended his hand. "You're the last one. Come aboard, come aboard."

"I'm Kelly," she said as she reached for his hand, and was surprised when her date held on and basically yanked her into the craft. Of course, he was wearing sensible boots with magnetic cleats, and maybe he had noticed she was a little hesitant on the ramp.

Olaf led her to a luxurious reclining seat pod, the sort of first-class accommodation which was equipped with a glass privacy cover that the occupant could activate to shut off all sound from the outside world. "Please strap in until you adjust to zero gravity after launch. You wouldn't want to kick somebody in the head by mistake."

"Wow, this is the nicest ship I've ever been on," Kelly gushed, smoothing her black dress over her thighs as she settled onto the plush cushions. The dress wasn't really meant for lying down, she reflected. The fashion designers expected you to take it off at that point of the evening. "Are all these pods taken by people going on the tour?"

"Yes, yes. We'll have time to chat after the launch. I have to take my place." He sounded much more excited than somebody going on a two hour cruise around the station, which Kelly took as a compliment to her appearance. Olaf vaulted into the pod next to Kelly, and she heard him mumble in the manner of somebody who had never quite mastered subvocalization, "Let's get out of here."

The ship lifted gently and passed soundlessly through the atmosphere retention field, and the seat pods all pivoted in unison, reorienting against the direction of the thrust. Acceleration was just noticeable at first, and then Kelly felt herself slowly sinking into the cushions as her full weight returned. But her weight continued to increase as they shot out the end of the station's cylindrical core.

"Aren't we going a bit too fast for a tour, Olaf?" Kelly ventured to ask her date, though her voice came out weakly since her chest felt like it was wrapped in heavy bands.

"Not now," he grunted, followed by a subvoc that she missed. Then he practically yelled, "I just said I wasn't talking to you, idiot. Yes, now, now, now!"

Kelly didn't have time to think before the glass isolation cover whooshed down over her seat and her body felt like all of its warmth was being sucked away by a giant pump.

"Libby," she cried through her implant. "Libby, I think I'm being kidnapped!"

A faint crackle sounded in her ears as the cold sank into her bones, then the reassuring voice of the station's Stryx librarian broke in with, "…jamming, but tracking. Please report status."

"I'm trapped in a seat pod, isolation cover down, freezing. I think I'm being put into stasis. It's an Eemas

42

date, check the records." Kelly banged her hands on the glass to no avail, but she saw Olaf dragging himself forward towards the front of the ship on his magnetic traction cleats. "Scramble fighters or something. Stop them."

"Fighters?" Despite her rapidly dimming consciousness, Kelly thought she could hear Libby chuckling. That's right, they don't have any, she remembered. "Don't worry, Kelly. We suspected there was a bride-stealing gang working the station. We just needed them to violate our regulations. I've already arranged for apprehension and retrieval, so help is on the way."

"You used me as date bait?" Kelly mumbled, lacking the energy to get angry about it as she felt herself drifting into sleep. "That wasn't very nice. Please turn off the freezer."

"You'll be safer in stasis, Kelly. We'll have to disable the ship. Sleep well." Libby closed the channel softly.

As everything faded to black, Kelly reflected that this, surely, was the new low point of her dating life.

Five

"Somebody's coming," Paul yelled into the jagged opening in the lifeboat hull, from which emitted an unending stream of curses and oddly colored wisps of smoke. The volume of curses increased even as the smoke died out, and a helmeted head with a dark visor poked out of the hull.

"Stupid auto-adjusting shield," Joe complained. He rapped the side of the welding helmet a couple of times with his glove-encased knuckles, then finally gave up and raised the visor manually. "Where's Killer?"

"Sleeping," Paul replied, and shrugged his shoulders at the pointless question. Beowulf, aka Killer, was a war dog, a genetically engineered cross between a mastiff and Huravian hound. The dog had chosen to stick with Joe when he left the mercenaries, and anybody who might have disagreed with the canine's choice had more sense than to argue with him.

Beowulf looked exactly like a war dog retired to junkyard duty. He weighed as much as a big man, drooled buckets, and mainly slept whenever Joe or Paul was around to keep watch. At the sound of his name, Beowulf's ears twitched and he opened his eyes. After a quick sniff and glance at the approaching robot, he made an elaborate show of curling up and going back to sleep in the nest of scrapped insulation he had arranged as a bed away from bed.

Joe left his cutting torches and gauntlets behind, pulled himself out of the lifeboat, and handed the helmet to Paul. Then he straightened out painfully and cast a critical eye over the strange amalgamation of parts that rolled up to him under its own power.

"This is a first," Joe said, as he untied the straps securing his leather welder's apron. "I've never had a robot come to junk itself before."

"How very droll," the robot responded with the pointed inflection peculiar to the Stryx. Its various articulated limbs undulated wildly about, like a blind octopus groping for the wheel on a submarine hatch. "About what I should have expected from a man who would take a second-hand dating subscription in barter."

"Oh, you're the guy from Eemas. That's a dirty trick you folks have, charging the full subscription price just to change the user profile!" Joe intended to work himself up for a tirade, but quickly became hypnotized watching the apparently uncontrollable spasms of the robot's extremities.

"I'm sure it was explained to you that the cost of the service is the research that goes into finding potential matches," the Stryx said, shifting to a tired monotone that suggested too much time spent doing customer service. "We offered you a very attractive alternative, and I understand you were quite enthusiastic about the terms."

"Yeah, well, my tug's right there, as you can see." Joe indicated the stubby salvage vessel that was built for the sole purpose of short-haul towing and orbital junk sifting. "Where's the exterior propulsion unit you guys promised?

I don't mind doing repo work, but I'll never catch a cabin cruiser, not even if you gave me the head start."

The robot ignored Joe, rolled up to the tug, and then right up its side onto the hull. "Let's go," it called.

"You're the propulsion system?" Joe asked in disbelief.

"They aren't getting any closer," the robot pronounced languidly, and its various limbs seemed to wilt as they sought anchoring spots on the hull. "Come on now, hotshot. Get the lead out." It snapped the commands with a momentary display of energy and knowledge of archaic human slang. "I didn't load myself down with all these extras to stand around yapping with a glorified trash collector."

"Alright, alright. Mind the shop, Paul, and no cutting until I get back." Joe gave the boy's shoulder a squeeze and then followed the Stryx to the tug. He stopped and shook his head at the little robot perched on the hull, then hauled himself up the ladder and into the cockpit. There was barely enough room for a human operator in the tug, which had been built for smaller humanoids and converted for human use.

The vessel was procured in a barter deal for a rather elaborate potbelly still which the former owner of the junkyard had employed to make pretty good moonshine. Joe had long since decided that he'd gotten the short end of the stick on that trade. Strapping himself into the command chair, he began the launch sequence by calling to station control for clearance, but the controls abruptly locked out.

"I'll do the talking and the flying if you don't mind." The robot spoke through his implants, sounding positively exhausted at this point. "How many G's can your body tolerate without permanent damage?"

In Joe's experience, nothing good ever came from responding to this type of question. However, his years in the mobile infantry had taught him the answer, and he decided to play it straight rather than leaving the robot to guess, especially since this particular Stryx didn't sound like it would be upset by accidentally turning Joe into a gelatinous mass. "I can take 5 G's for about thirty minutes, though I won't be worth much for a while when it cuts out. Or I can take 15 G's for around twenty seconds, but I'll pass out without a pressure suit."

"Passing out won't be necessary," the robot practically yawned the words in his ear. "Launch initiated."

The tug took off like it had been kicked by a Thurillian riding beast, blowing through the ionized field that kept the air in the hold, and out into the vacuum of the station core without pausing to check for traffic. There was a brief high G turn, and then Joe felt himself pressed back into the pilot's seat by a giant hand, though it was nowhere near as bad as some rapid assault landings he could recall, or strategic withdrawals for that matter.

Joe was impressed that so much thrust could be generated with the casually bolted-on attachments that made the little robot look like it had magnetized its casing and blundered through a scrap heap, but none of the biologicals fostered by the Stryx had a clue as to their patron's true technological limits. The robots gifted or bartered their fosterlings just enough technology to reach the stars, but generally left the different life forms to work out their own solutions to the problems they encountered in space.

The accelerometer on the tug's instrument panel held steady as the velocity continued to ramp up, already far beyond the speed the ship could have reached on its own even when it was new. Joe actually caught himself studying the forward sensor display for their fleeing quarry, but then he remembered that it had failed several months earlier and was replaying the same loop from memory over and over again. He tried to lift a hand to give the console a whack, but it was too much work, so he decided to trust the robot and promptly fell asleep like an old trooper.

Joe awoke to a bored voice intoning, "Target acquired, preparing to disable their propulsion system." He was still pressed down by a giant hand, but the instruments showed that velocity was dropping rapidly now.

"I can't see anything," he complained, looking through the forward port. "No visual contact."

"That's because I've turned the ship for deceleration," the Stryx responded. "It's also for your safety." There was a crackle of static and the field sensors on the console lit up with colors Joe hadn't seen in years, indicating that some high-energy weapon had been fired. Another of the robot's primitive looking attachments, no doubt.

"Please prepare for a brief period of discomfort as I match speeds." The robot offered the warning just as the invisible Thurillian beast that had kicked the tug out of the station took a seat on Joe's chest. He didn't pass out, quite, but a few more seconds would have done it. Then he was weightless, and a slight tremor passed through the tug as it gently bumped into something.

"Sharf vessel acquired," the Stryx droned in a monotone. "Please engage towing grapnels." Joe knew he was a little slow recovering from the hard deceleration, but it was downright mean-spirited of the robot to add, "It's the three blue buttons at the top left of your console. Press them in sequence."

"I know how to secure a tow," Joe responded irritably, but he hit the buttons quickly. The inelastic contact between the ships had been softer than anything he could have managed flying the tug manually, but the vessels would still be drifting slowly apart without the magnetic grapnels to hold them together. "Repo has been secured," he reported to the robot as the blue buttons turned green.

"Returning to Union Station." The Stryx finally sounded like it was waking up a little, and they began to move again. The accelerometer on the instrument panel settled at exactly 1 G as Joe's weight returned to normal. Apparently the robot saw no need to hurry back, or maybe it wanted to give Joe the most comfortable ride possible, which made him think of whoever was aboard the Sharf cabin cruiser.

"Hey, uh, Robot," Joe said, losing momentum as he realized he had never asked the Stryx its name. Well, it could have offered to tell me, he thought. "What about the passengers aboard that ship? Did the cabin take any damage from whatever you were shooting there?"

"Oh, please," the robot replied. "It's a civilian pleasure craft, not a battle cruiser. I could have stopped it by just grabbing the hull but this sorry excuse for a tug would have torn itself apart. Isn't somebody from your history famous for saying that with a good enough fulcrum, he could change a planet's orbit?"

"How should I know?" Joe replied with a shrug, musing over the fact that this Stryx had an ego. Maybe it was a juvenile. "I thought this was supposed to be a repo job. If you've vaporized their propulsion section, there goes ninety percent of the resale value."

"Your information was incorrect," the robot responded, returning to its prior languor. "The job was to retrieve a

Sharf cabin cruiser that departed Union Station without clearance in the commission of a crime. After we process the passengers, you are welcome to the ship and remaining contents for your little junk business."

"Oh," Joe said, not sure if he should be more thankful or insulted. Bringing the conversation to a close would probably be the best policy. "Well, if you don't need me for anything, I may as well catch up on my beauty sleep."

"If you ever do catch up, let me know," the robot replied. "I'd be happy to make the appropriate changes to your Eemas profile."

No question that was an insult, Joe thought, as he closed his eyes, but maybe the Stryx was having a bad day. Besides, didn't his father have a saying about looking a gift horse in the mouth? Joe knew about horses and their mouths from his childhood on the family ranch, not to mention cavalry stints on various worlds with technology bans. Even a toothless Sharf cabin cruiser was worth more than a herd of cow ponies. He smiled to himself at the thought that his dad would have called the robot a "pill," then he slipped into the dusty dreams of his youth.

Six

The first thing Kelly saw when she regained consciousness was a priority message from EarthCent which Libby had forwarded to her heads-up display.

congratulations stop

Congratulations? The end of congratulations? She moaned and blinked her eyes, trying to remember where she had been when she passed out, and then it came back to her in a rush. Date bait.

"Libby!" she called out angrily. "Come on, I know you can hear me."

"Welcome home," Libby's voice sounded smoothly in her head. "Sorry for the delay, I was just wrapping some things up. You're quite a hit with EarthCent, you know. From what I hear, they're going to upgrade the consulate to an embassy and give you a promotion to acting ambassador."

"Great, I'm sure I'll need it to pay for my rescue." Kelly grimaced as she lifted her head slowly and looked to both sides. She was still reclined in the seat pod from the excursion craft, but it was no longer in the ship. The cavernous space was probably a docking bay for a decent-sized vessel, but all she could see were a dozen seat pods just like the one she occupied, the isolation covers still in place.

The individual pods looked strangely out of context on the bare decking, and they trailed disconnected lengths of cable and tubing which witnessed how they had been mated with the excursion craft. Then a smallish robot rolled into view and did something to the external control panel on Kelly's pod. The glass cover rolled back and the Stryx version of an optimum human air mix filled her lungs.

"How do you feel, Consul Frank?" the robot politely inquired. "I hope you are suffering no ill effects from your brief stay in stasis."

"Fine, thank you," she mumbled automatically, realizing that Libby had retreated into the background for the time being. "Are you associated with the station library?"

"I'm a field agent for Eemas. I was responsible for your retrieval," the Stryx responded cheerily.

"Perhaps you can explain the coincidence of my two Eemas introductions turning out to be something other than dates?" Kelly said, putting on a professionally calm demeanor. Then she waited for a response as the silence stretched uncomfortably.

"Might I suggest that coincidence is unlikely in this case?" the robot finally offered in reply. The average Stryx tended to treat unwanted inquiries the same way human adults treat embarrassing questions from other people's children, with a mixture of good will and stonewalling. "Ah, the others are regaining consciousness. I really must see to them now," the robot exclaimed with a hint of relief, and rolled away to the nearest pod. Kelly swung her legs down to the deck, found she was sufficiently recovered to stand, and shuffled off in the robot's tracks.

"I've been bombarded by advertisements for your service as long as I've been on this station, and I've never seen a disclaimer stating that the Stryx might hijack a date for diplomatic or police purposes." Kelly spoke to the robot's back as it fiddled with the controls for the isolation cover of the next pod. A groggy young woman was trying to sit up behind the glass, and a moment later, the cover swung back with a hiss.

"Ugh, where am I?" the girl moaned. "The last thing I remember I was on a date at the Beer Garden in Little Europe. What happened?"

"You were abducted by a ring of bride-stealers," the robot answered, in what struck Kelly as an exaggeratedly mechanical voice. The color that had been creeping back into the girl's face beat a strategic retreat, and then returned in a red flood. "Fortunately, your EarthCent Consul was able to expose the operation, and the perpetrators have been deported from Union Station. Excuse me, I have others to release."

The robot rolled off to the next pod unit, and rather than follow it around the hold badgering it with questions it didn't appear inclined to answer, Kelly decided to wait with the girl, who looked like she was having a hard time shaking off the effects of stasis.

"It did say bride-stealers, didn't it?" the young woman asked, letting her head rest back on the cushion as she fought off a sudden wave of dizziness. Then she added in a tone of accusation, "I've heard some of those guys working the asteroid fields in this sector are pretty nice, and wealthy too."

"You can't mean you wanted to get kidnapped!" Kelly protested. "What if they had been slavers, or organ thieves?"

"But they weren't," the girl replied stubbornly. "The robot specifically said bride-stealers. That means there's a man waiting who could afford to pay for the abduction, and he's lonely enough to gamble on a strange woman who could turn out to be anyone. My own mother was stolen from an agricultural colony when she was just out of school, and she always said it was the best thing that ever happened to her."

"Oh, well excuse me for rescuing you," Kelly flared up. A shriek from the next pod over interrupted her, and she saw a woman striking at the robot with her bare hands. "Some women may not share your broad-minded views on abduction," she flung over her shoulder, as she shuffled over to calm the frantic woman.

"Twenty days! I've missed my connecting ship and the ticket was nonrefundable!" The woman moaned and rocked back and forth while sitting up in the pod, but her eyes were scanning and Kelly could see that she was using her implants to catch up. The robot was already rolling away to the next unit, and Kelly chased it down.

"Your bedside manner leaves a lot to be desired," she told it. "Let me do the talking."

"Yes, Consul," the robot replied meekly. Its attitude was so out of keeping with the personality of any Stryx she had ever encountered that Kelly got the feeling she was being manipulated by an amateur, but she didn't have the time or the heart to argue about it. Waking up the rest of the women and sending them on their way took another hour, but none of them seemed any worse for wear, other than the unplanned vacation in stasis. It quickly became clear that all of the victims were single women who had no family or friends on the station, and more than one was quite annoyed with Kelly for sticking her nose in other people's business.

"You just wait right there," she hurled at the robot, as it tried to stealthily roll away after opening the last pod. Surprisingly, the Stryx didn't even argue, but stood motionless while Kelly explained the situation to the last woman revived and offered the help of the consulate.

"Has the consulate started a matchmaking service?" the woman asked hopefully. When Kelly shook her head, the woman just looked disgusted and stumbled away.

Kelly turned and addressed the robot. "Now, you have some explaining to do. But first, what should I call you?"

"My English name?" the Stryx mused. "I rather fancy Jeeves, if it's all the same to you."

"Fine, Jeeves. So who made the decision to drag me into the middle of this bride-stealing mess, and what's the connection between Eemas and EarthCent?"

"There is no direct connection, Consul, but surely you know that we Stryx enjoy a highly cooperative culture," the robot replied evasively.

"Then what's the connection between Eemas and station management?" she asked.

"Ah, that's rather complicated. But I can tell you that two of the women on that ship were introduced to the bride-stealers through Eemas, and as soon as we suspected what was going on, we had to act to defend our business model." Jeeves sounded indignant rather than defensive, and Kelly wondered if he was a stakeholder in the dating service.

"So why didn't you just deport the guys and confiscate their ship?"

"You know that we don't like imposing rules on other species, and bride-stealing is a widespread practice in many cultures. It doesn't always include prior negotiations."

"And I entered into this how?" Kelly asked.

"You fit the profile," Jeeves responded. "That made the date legitimate for both parties, and we do have a guaranty to uphold."

"I what?" Kelly slapped the robot's head and hurt her hand. "You think I'm so desperate to find a man that I want to get kidnapped?"

"In any case, as an EarthCent employee, your implants are diplomatic quality, and of course, you authorized remote monitoring when you signed your employment contract," the Stryx continued unperturbed. "By taking you without your prior consent, the bride-stealers violated your diplomatic immunity, which gave us an excuse to step in."

"Hold on a sec," Kelly protested, with the feeling she was getting too much new information all at once. "What was that bit about authorizing remote monitoring of my implants? Do you mean you have me bugged?"

"Strange how nobody from your world ever reads the end user license agreements," Jeeves said by way of an answer. "This must have been the first time your implants were accessed remotely, or you would have been aware of it. The EarthCent agreement stipulates that the employee will be notified of any remote monitoring within one pay period. This conversation is being entered in the records as proof that notification was made."

"Just wait a minute, and stop changing the subject," Kelly demanded, trying to recall which question the robot was evading. But the whole situation was too confusing and she just wanted to get home and go to sleep. "I'm not through with you," she concluded lamely.

"You've had a strenuous day and you need to rest," Jeeves soothed her. "After a good night's sleep, I hope you will see this experience in a new light. Remember, Eemas knows you better than you know yourself." After invoking the tagline from the ads, the Stryx began rolling towards the exit.

Kelly followed the robot in silence as she formed and discarded new lines of questioning. When they reached the corridor, Jeeves patiently waited for Kelly to choose her direction, which was towards the lift tube bank, and then he headed off the opposite way. Just before the tube door closed, it occurred to her to yell at the vanishing robot, "Hey! Does whatever you call what just happened count as a date on my subscription?"

Jeeves, who could probably pick up the vibrations of a butterfly landing on a leaf on a remote ag deck, somehow failed to hear the question and rolled along his merry way.

Seven

None of the mercenaries who had fought behind Joe's leadership would have believed he could ever be so nervous, but speaking to a roomful of children was not the sort of challenge he relished. He was only there because Paul had practically begged Joe to appear as his parent or guardian for the career show-and-tell, one of the group classes the Stryx offered so the children could socialize.

Despite Paul's usual shyness, he was eager to introduce his stand-in parent to the class, and Joe waited his turn in the corridor for Paul to come out and get him. The door slid open and a well-dressed woman stumbled out, swabbing the sweat from her face with a handkerchief.

"That was brutal," she muttered to Joe. "It made my dissertation defense seem like a cake walk."

"What do you do," he asked her curiously.

"I'm an astrophysicist with the Stryx singularity prediction labs," she answered with a groan. "The questions those kids ask. Nobody warned me. Well, the shoe will be on the other foot when my little angels come looking for dinner tonight!"

Joe wilted a little, and began to wonder how mad Paul could really get if he just made a run for it. He was shifting his weight to the balls of his feet when the door slid open again and he saw the boy's face.

"Hey, Joe. What are you doing? It's time," Paul said, and made a beckoning gesture.

Joe drew himself up, squared his shoulders, and followed Paul into the class. It turned out to be a friendly-looking room with some sort of grass on the floor, and he couldn't tell if it was real or fake. There were more than forty kids there, ages ranging from around eight to fourteen, along with at least twenty little robots of a type he had either never seen or never paid attention to before. Paul led him to the front of the room and launched right into his introduction.

"This is Joe. He's been filling in for my parents since I was eight. I live with him in the crew module of an ice harvester down at Mac's Bones, which he won in a card game. He teaches me how to use all sorts of cool tools, like torches and molecular shears. He's not going to give a speech like that physicist, so you can just ask him questions and stuff. Joe?

"Hi, kids," Joe began, trying to sound confident and ending up almost yelling. "Uh, Paul has told me how great the school is and how hard you all work. He already told you that I own Mac's Bones, so that makes me a sort of a recycling engineer." Joe improvised the last bit on the spur of the moment, hoping that it would keep him from being entirely outclassed by the other parents. "Any questions?"

Every hand in the room shot up, including some metallic ones, and for the second time in as many minutes, Joe fought a sudden impulse to flee. He stared at the sea of eager little faces for a moment, and then thought he recognized a small girl and pointed in her direction.

"How much do you make selling junk?" she demanded. Joe recognized too late the older of the two flower girls.

"Uh, it varies a lot from cycle to cycle. And sometimes I get paid for doing nothing, like last cycle, when I got twenty-five hundred Stryx creds as an order cancellation penalty."

"Wow!" Blythe marveled. "That's a lot!"

"And of course, I mainly do barter," Joe added in relief, thinking this might not be so bad after all.

"Barter is better," the kids all answered in chorus, and the hands shot back up again.

"Yes, in the front there, with the green hair."

"How long did you have to go to school to become a recycling engineer?" asked a gangly looking boy, who was around the same age as Paul.

"Yeah, about that, uh, I'm, uh, self-taught. Next question?"

"Did you ever find a dead body in an old spaceship?" asked a little boy, his eyes round with excitement. All of the children ooh'ed.

"Uh, no," Joe lied, figuring it was just a white lie since they were asking about the junk business and not his fighting career. There was a collective exhalation of disappointment from the class, so he decided to embellish a little. "But I've had to clean up my share of sudden decompression stains." The kids all ooh'ed again, and up came the hands.

"Yes, with the black hat."

"Why is it called Mac's Bones?"

"Oh. Well, 'Mac' is me, my whole name is Joe McAllister. And 'Bones' is sort of a tradition from Earth, where junkyards were often called bone yards, because they are full of the bones of old vehicles. Does that make sense?"

"Are you married?" asked a little girl in the moment of silence that followed.

"Uh, no, I'm not married," Joe answered. He looked for another hand to pick, but the little girl was too fast.

"Why not?"

"I, uh, I just never found the right woman. Or maybe she never found me," Joe stumbled through the explanation.

"Do you have any children, other than Paul, I mean?" asked another girl without waiting to be picked.

"I, no, Paul's it right now."

"Don't you LIKE children?" asked a different little boy.

"Uh, yeah. Of course I like children," answered Joe, who was beginning to sense that the kids were circling like sharks, or maybe piranhas. "My dog likes children too."

"Ooh, you have a dog? What's his name? How big is he? Has he bitten any robbers?"

"His name is Beowulf, but I call him Killer. He's about as big as I am, but he's shaped differently. He hasn't bitten any robbers because they run like crazy as soon as they see him."

"Why didn't you bring the dog with you?" asked a little girl.

"When I'm here, he has to guard the junkyard," Joe explained.

"Oh," the children all chorused in disappointment. A few of them eyed Joe speculatively, as if they were thinking of requesting a personnel change, but apparently that fell outside the guidelines of proper conduct for a parental show-and-tell. Joe noticed again that some of the little robots had a pincer raised, so he pointed in the direction of a couple of them and said, "Yes? The little robot, er, Stryx in front?"

"If you're in the recycling business, why do people call it junk?" asked the little robot, in the squeakiest, most mechanical voice Joe had ever heard coming from a Stryx.

"Ah, that's a good question. I guess we call it junk because when it comes to me, nobody wants it any more, or at least they don't want to spend the money and the time to make it into something they could easily sell. I usually buy stuff for the scrap value, what I can sell the materials for after taking it apart. But sometimes, I'll pay more or barter for something that I can fix up."

"Thank you," the little robot responded, and Joe pointed to the Stryx behind it.

"How do you ensure that the ships and equipment you buy aren't stolen?"

"Oh, uh, that's a good question too," Joe replied automatically to gain time. "I, uh, well, for entire ships, I always check with the station librarian to see if they're listed as stolen. Most of the galactic civilizations don't code the individual parts, so if the markings on the hull are painted over and the ship's transponder is gone, I'm sort of in the dark. But you have to remember that the salvage value is pretty low for most of this stuff and there's not a lot of local demand, so it doesn't make sense for criminals and pirates to steal things just to sell them for scrap."

"Thank you," the second little robot responded, and Joe reluctantly pointed at the third.

"Do you buy some things without knowing what they are?"

"All the time," he answered, relieved to get a softball question. "Some of the junk I get has been in space so long that even the station librarian doesn't recognize the language stamped on the parts. And sometimes I get stuff that comes from outside of Stryx space. Junk has a way of moving around."

"But what if you cut into a gravitational vortex mine leftover from the Founding War, or opened a tri-folded universe that sucked in the whole station, or even the whole galaxy?" the little Stryx followed up. All the children ooh'ed again, and Joe would have sworn that the little robots sat up straighter as well.

"I, uh, I try to be careful," Joe answered lamely. "Besides, anybody who could seal up a galaxy-eating thingy in a can probably wouldn't lose track of it, and I doubt it would be anything I could cut open either. Little children, er, young Stryx, shouldn't worry about things like that. It can give you nightmares."

"Well, that's time," Paul exclaimed, coming to Joe's rescue. "If anybody wants to come meet Beowulf, just ask me later and I'll bring him out to the park."

"Thank you, Mr. Joe," the children chorused.

"Thank you, kids," Joe replied, giving a weak wave and practically running for the exit. It wasn't until he was in the corridor that he realized how relieved he was to be out of the room. A woman with a collapsible easel and a stack of posters, the first of which showed a large pie chart, was waiting in the hall.

"Rough audience, huh?" she asked sympathetically. "What do you do?"

"I'm a recycling, I mean, junk man."

"Oh, kids like stuff like that. Do you have a dog?"

Joe nodded in the affirmative.

"I wish we had a dog," the woman continued mournfully. "I'm an economic historian. How am I going to explain monetary policy and fiat currency to kids who believe that barter is better?"

The door slid open, a little girl came out, and she looked up and down the hall.

"Where's Daddy?" the girl asked the woman.

"Daddy ran away," her mother answered grimly, then she picked up her easel and followed her daughter into the room.

Eight

Armed with twenty creds from petty cash, Kelly installed her nose plugs, snorted through them once or twice to activate the filters, and set off for the importers market. The embassy had recently been inundated by complaints from human merchants that the station was being flooded with counterfeit kitchen gadgets, and even worse, that they were junk. So not only were the legitimate merchants getting undercut on pricing, they were worried that Earth's carefully nurtured brand value was being destroyed.

The humans on Union Station referred to the importers market as the "Shuk", after the famous Jerusalem market with its piles of goods and noisy, often aggressive, vendors. But the Shuk was probably the busiest meeting point for species that could tolerate the atmosphere on the deck, with or without the aid of filters, and human vendors occupied less than five percent of the floor area.

There were no corridors or rooms in the Shuk. The deck was wide open except for the structural members, or spokes, that pierced the floor and ceiling at regular intervals on all of the decks. Food stalls were mixed in amongst the dry goods booths with vendors selling everything from rugs to personal weaponry. But for the main part, the Shuk merchants specialized in selling imported goods from their home worlds to buyers from other species.

Even the least observant visitor to the human area of the Shuk would quickly realize that the main products for sale were gadgets and games. As a backwards world only recently arrived on the galactic stage, Earth couldn't export any high technology products, since they looked like crude antiques in comparison to the poorest offerings from the next world up in the pecking order.

But the galaxy was full of game players, and it turned out that human war games translated well to many cultures. And then there were the flashy kitchen gadgets, a phenomenon unique to Earth that had caught the eyes and imaginations of many species.

Kelly heard that the most complicated and expensive gadgets had even started selling to aliens who didn't eat, in any normal sense of the word. Some saw the gleaming stainless steel hardware with gears, spinning handles and pincers as a form of primitive artwork. Others might have been purchasing can openers as torture devices. The important thing was that Earth had finally begun to move towards a more balanced trade, but it was being undermined by counterfeits.

Kelly quickly located the stand of Peter Hadad, one of the Earth Merchants Council members who had attended the meeting at the embassy the previous week. Peter was the proprietor of Kitchen Kitsch, a sprawling collection of shelves and tables manned by his extended family, including at least one daughter who obviously shared his lung capacity.

"Can openers, bottle openers, cork screws and juicers. That's right, Kitchen Kitsch has them all at the best prices on the station. Did I say on the station? I meant in the galaxy. Come see the miraculous egg slicer in action. Kitchen Kitsch offers demonstrations every ten minutes on the hour. Can openers, can openers, can openers." The girl's sharp alto cut through her tenor and bass competition like a Ginsu knife through a tin can.

"Hi, there. I'm Kelly Frank from the embassy," Kelly introduced herself to the waif of admirable volume. The girl was short like her father, with the same black hair, black eyes, and a humorous, animated face. Her colorful garb might have been a traditional costume from an old Earth nation, or it could have been assembled from closeout pieces bought on the cheap. Nobody would know the difference.

"I'm Shaina," the girl replied, and she bumped Kelly with an outstretched elbow, apparently intended as friendly greeting. "My dad told me to watch for you. He's down on the docking deck trying to clear up some problems with a shipment, so I'll be taking you around if that's okay."

"I'm sure that will be fine," Kelly said with a smile. "I'm not taking you away from the business?"

"Briiiiiiindaaaaaa," the young woman called, and a girl who could have been a clone who left the vat one or two years after Shaina appeared out of nowhere. "You're on, girl. I'm taking the diplomat lady around on a counterfeits tour."

Brinda grinned happily, threw Kelly an elbow, and started right in with the same piercing alto. "Nutcrackers, nutcrackers, nutcrackers. Kitchen Kitsch has the best collection of genuine Earth nutcrackers this side of the universe. Whisks great and small. Whisk your eggs, whisk your potatoes, we have them all. Nutcrackers, nutcrackers, nutcrackers."

Shaina led Kelly away through the labyrinthine paths between piles of goods, formal stalls, and random collections of display cases and tables. One of the obvious differences between the Union Station Shuk and its outdoor equivalents on worlds around the galaxy was the lack of inclement weather. Without that threat, there was no need for roofs, or for walls to support them.

Locking up wasn't necessary when the vendors took time off, as the Stryx offered zoned motion alarms throughout the deck, backed up by cameras and maintenance bots. The sharp-eyed vendors were proof against most shoplifters when their stalls were open, so the main theft problem was pickpockets operating in the thick press of the crowds during the high traffic periods.

"I'm sure my father told you that we police ourselves against counterfeits," Shaina began her explanation of the situation. "There are plenty of humans here who would happily sell the junk for a quick profit, but we run them off if they try it."

Although there were no barriers or lines on the floor, it was obvious when they crossed the border between the human area of the Shuk into the next section, which happened to be populated by Dollnick merchants. As they penetrated deeper into the narrow alleys formed by the vertical carousels favored by Dollnicks for displaying merchandise, Kelly's translation implant was overwhelmed by the ceaseless cries of the vendors, and eventually it reached its noise limit and stopped trying. Without the translation and simultaneous cancellation, it sounded to Kelly like they were striding through a tropical jungle pierced by birdcalls and screeching monkeys.

Shaina moved a little closer to Kelly as they walked, and pitched her voice lower, so she wouldn't be competing directly with the higher frequency chatter. "But the aliens, some of them only care about making a quick score off the tourist trade. Pretty much any non-humans you see selling Earth products are selling fakes. It's only in the retail stores on the residential decks that you'll find legitimate Earth stuff in alien-owned stores, and even then, sometimes it's just higher quality fakes."

They halted in front of one of the vertical carousels and Shaina grabbed the edge of a shelf, which brought the slow revolutions to a halt. A dazzling collection of shiny devices that Kelly wouldn't have recognized in a kitchen were displayed on trays, along with the blue/green globe logo that was the trademarked emblem of the Earth Export League.

"Here, try this," Shaina suggested. She handed Kelly a complex mechanism that looked a little like two spoons with raised spikes in their bowls, held apart from each other in a heavy "U" shaped guide with a wheel on the end like an ancient printing press.

"Uh, what is it?" Kelly hefted the device in both hands, not even sure how to hold it.

"It's a nutcracker, of course. Don't you like nuts? Here, try this one. I keep my pockets full for our demos."

Kelly accepted the hefty Brazil nut, studied the nutcracker, and finally placed the nut between the two opposing spoons. "Is that it?" she asked, as the tall Dollnick vendor, attracted by the halted carousel, appeared at her side. A couple of other shoppers stopped to look on as well, since visiting the Shuk was as much about entertainment as shopping.

"Yup. Now hold the handles of the spoony things in one hand and turn the wheel with the other."

Kelly turned the wheel, which thanks to the fine threading on the screw, went quite easily. But rather than cracking the nut open, the two spoons slowly deformed, as if they were melting in high heat or being manipulated by a mentalist.

"That's enough, lady!" Kelly froze at the bellow as her translation implant came back to life. A giant Dollnick was glowering down at her. At least, she hoped it was only glowering. "You broke it, you buy it."

Kelly reflexively let go of the failed nutcracker with one hand and began fishing in her pouch for money, but Shaina elbowed her way past and jabbed a finger up into the chest of the Dollnick, who towered over her.

"Now you listen to me, you seller of schlock. You're giving all of us merchants a bad name with your counterfeit trash." Shaina ripped into the vendor with her head tilted back as far as her neck would allow so she could stare him in the face. "Show me your Dolly license. NOW!"

The Dollnick, who had appeared ready to eat Kelly for lunch, now backed away, crossing all four of his arms in front of his chest in a gesture of pacification.

"I didn't realize she was with you, Hadad," he pleaded. "I don't want any trouble with you. I just bought this stuff at the docks. The ship captain assured me that it was all genuine Earth cargo."

"Like hell," Shaina snarled at the Dollnick, jutting out her elfin chin. "I'm making a citizen's confiscation for station management. Do you want to make something of it? Do you?"

The Dollnick mumbled something about "Stryx pets," and hastily reactivated the carousel to carry the rest of the counterfeit kitchen gadgets on the shelf out of view. He didn't protest when Shaina tapped Kelly on the arm and motioned her away.

"You have to keep them off balance," the girl explained to Kelly as they continued their inspection tour. "The Dollnicks live in a rigidly hierarchical society based on traditional combat, though I've heard it has as much to do with putting on a show as with actually fighting to the death. In any case, they only challenge each other when they are confident of victory, so they aren't very good at up-close confrontations with other species who are used to getting in each other's faces."

"You mean that hulking monster backed off because he thought you were going to beat him up?" Kelly asked in amazement.

"I'm sure he didn't think it so much as feel it in his bones, that's how social conditioning works." Shaina broke into a wide smile. "Maybe I would have gotten away with a knee kick and toppled him. They come from a low-gravity planet so they aren't as stable as they look. We learned some pretty good tricks in Stryx school."

"You know, this nutcracker thing really looked like it could break rocks before I started turning the screw," Kelly commented. She held it up for a closer look as they wound their way through the Dollnick stands.

"That's just the problem," Shaina said angrily, as she took the mangled nutcracker from Kelly and bent back one of the spoons to retrieve the hard nut. "We sell the same nutcracker, except ours is really imported from old Sweden, and you can crack rocks with it. Of course, it costs us more than ten times as much as this fake made out of pot metal with a twenty-atom-thick layer of chrome. That Dolly would have offered it for five creds, maybe settled for two, while the real thing costs us six creds wholesale!"

71

"Who would buy from him a second time?"

"Nobody, but he doesn't care because only tourists would buy his garbage in the first place, and they aren't coming back again anyway. No, that's not entirely true either, because a lot of the aliens buying fancy mechanical gadgets are just using them as decorations. If you hung this thing on the wall and never touched it, it would hold up just fine. Oh, these are great," Shaina interrupted herself, grabbing at a shelf displaying wrist watches on one of the many glittering carousels in what looked like a high-end jewelry shop.

"Oh, those are beautiful. I wish I could afford something like that." Kelly pictured herself with one of the watches on her wrist while she was wearing her black dress, and sighed.

The girl gave Kelly a curious look of pity, though whether it was for her financial situation or her ignorance of prices, Kelly wasn't sure. "Anybody can afford one of these watches. They're brilliant, and they aren't copies. Try one on."

"But I thought that mechanical wrist watches were one of the few exports we had that were entirely safe from counterfeits," Kelly said. "Libby told me that with all the little gears and springs, it's just not worth the effort for advanced civilizations that don't have any similar technology or skills to use for a starting point. But look, there's no watch face on any of these so you can even see all of the internal parts working." Kelly took a watch from the display and modeled it on her wrist.

"That watch looks like it was made for you, Human," boomed the voice of a Dollnick, who at nearly twice Kelly's height, made the last vendor look like a child. "For a friend of the little one, I will make you a price of fifty creds."

Kelly shook her head sadly, thinking of the twenty creds she had taken from petty cash to buy fakes, and the three creds in small coins in her pouch, which were all she had to her name until payday.

"Hey, Rupe," Shaina greeted the giant, whose mass must have been greater than that of her entire family, with plenty of neighbors thrown in. "Make it two creds and I'll buy it for her."

"Two creds! You would steal the food from my nestlings, little one. Perhaps I could come down to forty creds, since your friend and the watch are so obviously suited to each other."

"Forty creds would buy a gross of those watches," the girl countered, her eyes smiling joyously. "Do you want I should get a batch and go into the business? But I do agree that the band matches her hair, so I would consider offering you two and a half creds."

"I swear on the Ka of my dear, transcended sire, that I would lose money selling you that watch for two and a half creds," Rupe proclaimed theatrically, and piled all four of his hands on the region of his chest that Kelly assumed housed his enormous heart. "But I was only kidding with you of course. Shall we call it ten creds and rub elbows?"

"Three creds and this imported Brazil nut." Shaina made her final offer, holding up the slightly damaged nut, which looked truly enormous in contrast to her small thumb and forefinger.

"Done," the Dollnick replied, and the two bumped elbows, the girl stretching hers up above her shoulder,

Rupe crouching a bit to make contact using his lower set of arms. "Let me get you a box."

"Three creds and a used Brazil nut?" Kelly stared at the girl wide-eyed. "Can you renegotiate the lease on my apartment for me? I swear I'm never buying anything again without you along."

Shaina blushed and kicked at the deck plates, embarrassed by the praise. "It's nothing, you just have to grow up around it and know what things are worth. Like Libby told you, nobody could really build a true mechanical watch as cheap as Rupe is selling them. The mechanically accurate counterfeits of the luxury names actually come from Earth. The box he's getting and the nice wrist band are worth more than the watch. Those aren't real gears, you know. It's just a mass produced high-res display showing video of a working mechanical watch with superimposed hands."

"Oh, it's still beautiful," Kelly said, only a little disappointed to learn she wasn't getting a genuine knock-off of a true luxury item.

"Yeah, they're pretty popular, despite the fact that nobody other than humans has any real use for them."

"What do you mean?" Kelly asked. "I know that we're the only ones using twenty-four hour days and sixty-minute hours, but surely a high-tech watch like this could be easily set to any time system."

"It's not that," Shaina said and gave Kelly another odd look. "All of the aliens I've ever been around keep time in their heads, and even for humans, it's easier to check an implant than to look at your wrist. Watches are jewelry."

Rupe delivered a handsome black box to go with the watch, which Kelly decided to wear, and Shaina handed over the Brazil nut and three creds.

"Thanks, Rupe. This is Kelly, our acting ambassador. I'm taking her to the Dinery to check out the counterfeits."

"Why is she pretending to be an ambassador?" Rupe asked. But then he realized that the human might be embarrassed by the question and added, "Never mind. Enjoy the Dinery, and don't let those Frunge thieves get the better of you."

"I won't, Rupe. See you around."

"Nice meeting you, and I'm really not pretending," Kelly couldn't help herself from protesting, as Shaina laughed and led her away. They soon crossed another invisible boundary, where the Dollnick merchants were replaced by Frunge, whose characteristic vine-like hair made their stands look like overgrown shrubbery. After negotiating several aisles of displays featuring the wing sets which made the Frunge a household name on most resort worlds, they came to a section that was given over to anything that could cut or stab.

From paring knives to great battle axes, if it had an edge, it was available for sale. Some of the pieces with intricate gold filigree inlays looked like they belonged in museums, and one vendor was even set up as a smithy, selling customized suits of armor. Shaina shouldered her way through the crowded aisles between the displays until they arrived at an impressive spread of tables featuring Earth cutlery, especially chef's knives sets, along with artistic wooden blocks to hold the implements.

"This is it," Shaina muttered out of the side of her mouth and gestured with her head. "Good, they're busy with other customers. What jumps out at you about this stuff?" she asked, holding a carving knife up for Kelly's inspection.

"Well, it all looks really high quality," Kelly answered honestly. "My friend Donna has an expensive knife set, and these blades look kind of dull like hers, not shiny like you would expect from fakes."

"How about the brand?" Shaina prompted her.

"Dinery," Kelly read the odd sticker that appeared on all of the cutlery available for sale. "Why are the letters spread out funny like that, and how did they make the letters on the sticker look engraved?"

Shaina took another look around to see if they'd been spotted yet, and then peeled back the sticker, revealing the "Made in Germany" mark stamped into the blade. The sticker was nothing more than a white label with spaces cut out to let the letters "d in er y" appear.

"This is the other side of counterfeiting, where the customers know they are buying knock-offs. Take the knives home, peel the stickers, and you can impress your dinner guests."

"Ouch, that's really low," Kelly marveled. One of the Frunge manning the booth finally looked up, and noticing the women, slid swiftly in their direction on its root-like feet.

"I have a budget of twenty creds to acquire some proof for a formal report. Can we afford one of these cutlery sets?" Kelly whispered to Shaina. The girl grinned in reply and turned to the approaching Frunge.

"May the rains nourish your seedlings, may the suns harden their bark," she addressed the Frunge formally, then immediately launched into the bargaining. "I'll give you a cred for the big set if you throw in those napkin holders."

Five minutes later, the women left carrying two full sets of chef's knives and various throw-ins, which taken together made an eight cred dent in Kelly's budget.

"These knives really aren't that bad, they hold a decent edge," Shaina admitted, sounding a little guilty. "But they've never been closer to Germany than I have, and I was born and raised here."

They continued browsing and shopping for another hour, examining fakes and occasionally acquiring an example piece. Finally, Kelly realized she had to carry it all back to the office and called it quits. The girl led Kelly to the nearest lift tube.

"I can't thank you enough for all of the help, and I was serious about what I asked before. Maybe I can pay you a commission to bargain for me next time I have to buy something big?"

"Barter is better," the girl replied automatically. "If you can figure out a way to slow down these counterfeiters, you'll be helping us all."

"At least let me pay you back for the watch. I didn't even spend the whole twenty creds," Kelly protested.

"No, no." Shaina waved away the proffered money. "We don't believe in something for nothing in the Shuk. Let me know if you need anything from me or my father. We're fighting for our business here."

"I'll do my best," Kelly replied, and on accepting the bags the girl had been carrying, found she could barely lift her arm for an elbow bump before entering the capsule.

Nine

The gravity on the inner agricultural deck was barely higher than that of the junkyard, so Beowulf was able to snag a Frisbee that might have soared just over his nose if he'd been on Earth. On either side of the grassy band of parkland were orchards of fruit trees, narrow fields of vegetables and manicured rows of flowers. The apiaries rotated their bees through the sections of the inner agricultural rings set aside for the flora of compatible worlds.

Most foodstuffs on the station were imported as dry or frozen, of course. Only the giant colony ships carried a full complement of the flora and fauna needed to seed a new world and feed an isolated population. But there was always a market for fresh fruits and vegetables, and many of the station's biologicals benefitted from spending time in the great outdoors, even with the low metal ceilings and artificial lighting.

Beowulf trotted back to the picnic with his prize and waited patiently for Joe or Paul to notice him. But it was the woman accompanying them who glanced up first, and she did a double-take. Then she rose to her feet, pushing herself up off of Joe's shoulder.

"This is exactly what I was talking about," she said, and pointed at Beowulf. "None of you guys care about what anybody else thinks!"

Joe and Paul turned and looked at the Frisbee clamped in Beowulf's mouth, and also at the Jack Russell terrier hanging onto the rim of the Frisbee by its teeth and growling as best it could under the circumstances. The terrier's legs were churning away in a frantic dog paddle, as if trying to convince the world that it was suspended in the air through its own efforts. Beowulf didn't appear to notice the little dog at all.

"Bad dog," Joe said, though both Paul and Beowulf could tell from his tone that he didn't mean anything by it. "Drop it."

Beowulf let go of the Frisbee, and the Jack Russell took off running with it, making incredible time on his bandy legs.

"They're just playing, Trisha," Joe objected. "You take everything too seriously." The four of them watched the Jack Russell as it grew smaller and higher, and then suddenly it disappeared into the ceiling lights. The curvature of the inner decks was more noticeable than on the outer levels, where the pseudo-gravity generated by the station's spin was higher as well.

The air on the agricultural decks was rich in oxygen content, and the station plumbing used it as a buffer for the atmospheric recycling systems. It wasn't necessary, just elegant, and the Stryx, despite their nearly unlimited energy resources, prided themselves on taking the time to engineer things with style. The first Stryx joke Joe had ever heard went something like, "When you live forever, entropy gets to be a drag." As with all robot jokes he had to ask for an explanation, which made sense, but not humor.

"And you never took anything seriously enough, including me!" Trisha rebutted Joe. "I'm not saying the dog is the only reason it didn't work out between us, but neither of you are as smart as you think you are."

Beowulf cocked his head and gave Trisha a questioning look. Why was she lumping him in with Joe?

"Don't you remember going to the market with Killer?" Joe asked. "He didn't just shop by smell, he read the prices on the slates, and if he thought the stall owners were colluding, he'd go nose to nose and stare them down. If that dog had opposable thumbs and the gift of speech, he'd be unstoppable. Trust me, he's smarter than both of us."

"I remember you taking Beowulf to the market and him intimidating all of the poor vendors. And that's just like the two of you as well." Trisha grabbed Beowulf's head in both hands, and staring down into his innocent brown eyes, addressed the dog. "If you're so smart, you find him a woman. I can see my advice isn't needed around here." Then she turned about abruptly and began stalking off towards the lifts.

"C'mon, Trisha. Wait up," Joe pleaded. He grabbed at her arm, missed, and took a couple jogging steps through the grass to catch up. "You know I respect your judgment and I'd be happy to take your friend on a date. But I have this Eemas subscription to use up, and you wouldn't believe what I went through to get it squared away."

"Do you really believe that an overgrown alien computer can do a better job at matchmaking than a woman who knows you intimately?" Trisha glared and crossed her arms, even as she continued walking rapidly towards the lifts.

"Of course not," Joe lied, wincing at the memory of the half a dozen dates Trisha had talked him into after unilaterally deciding it would be better if the two of them were just friends. "But the Eemas thing was a barter deal, you know? I can't just throw it out, and it turns out I can't sell it either, so I'm basically stuck."

"I think you're hoping that Eemas studies your profile and sets you up with the same woman you got on your last outing," Trisha said cruelly, making Joe ask himself for the twentieth time why he had told her the story. The failed date had seemed pretty funny the day after when he told everybody he knew, but Trisha and his acquaintances hadn't stopped razzing him since. It made him miss his mercenary days, when he carried enough weaponry to engage a platoon, and nobody gambled on his good nature.

"If anybody knows that's not true, it's you," Joe said as she stepped into the lift, but he didn't really expect an answer, and Trisha lived up to his expectations. "You're really so mad that you're going home early?"

"Does this answer your question?" Trisha asked, arching an eyebrow and stating her destination to the lift tube.

Joe turned away as the tube door slid shut, and began calling for Beowulf, who was nowhere in sight. Unfortunately, the dog could out-robot a Stryx in an "I can't hear you contest," when he didn't feel like coming. Of course, Paul had gone with the dog, so Joe jogged off in the direction the little terrier had disappeared with the Frisbee.

The truth of the matter was that Trisha liked Joe and the dog well enough, it was Paul who drove her to distraction during their brief experiment with living together. The boy was too quiet and self-contained, and he wanted no part of a substitute mother. Joe insisted that Paul was doing fine and there was no need to seek professional help or to send him back to Earth for a more "normal" environment. In this, Paul and Beowulf concurred wholeheartedly.

Joe kept calling Beowulf as he jogged up the deck, an exercise reminiscent of workouts on long-range troop carriers, which included a centrifugal track to keep the soldiers from losing bone mass. Eventually Beowulf burst from a field of tomato vines and barked the signal for him to follow. Joe charged after the dog, running between the rows of fruit laden vines with their characteristic reek. An unreasonable fear gripped his heart that the boy had run afoul of some defective piece of farm equipment.

Just before the war dog and the old soldier reached the bulkhead at the edge of the field, they came upon Paul crouched on his haunches, studying something with rapt attention. He was staring at the ground, below the dense green leaves and heavy tomatoes that ran the color gamut from pale green to deep red. Joe followed the boy's eyes and saw a Stygian black ground vine winding about the thick stems of the plants, its leaves undulating as if ruffled by a breeze, except the air was still.

"What is it, Paul?" Joe demanded. He was relieved to find the boy whole and on his feet, and angry to find himself so out of breath.

Paul didn't answer and he seemed to be in a trance. Beowulf whined at the boy, and then growled at the black vines. Joe strode over to the boy and crouched next to him for a closer look.

"What is it, Paul? You've seen this stuff before?"

"We had it in school last year. It's on the prohibited list."

"Do you remember what they called it? What it's for?"

"It's not natural, and it only grows around plants it can feed off. It's some kind of advanced alien tech that alters the plants it attacks without harming them, but the biologicals that eat the plants or their fruit get dosed with a drug. I remember because it's used to cheat at gaming somehow," Paul added.

"You didn't touch it, did you?"

"You think I'd risk touching something that can mess with my game?" the boy asked in surprise. "Anyway, are you going to destroy it?"

"It's not mine to destroy. Maybe the stuff is good for something. It's hard to believe anything could grow here without the Stryx knowing about it, but it would be impossible to see this stuff from the ceiling cameras because the canopy is too dense. I'll notify Gryph and you can run up to the EarthCent embassy and tell them to check up on the owner of the field, since tomatoes are a human crop. Have you been recording?"

"I forgot to activate storage," Paul admitted. "I'll record a few seconds now and upload it for them." He turned back again, crouched, and looking closely at one of the moving vines, triggered his optical implant to work in reverse. The implant began collecting the image data from his optic nerve, rather than projecting a virtual heads-up holographic display, its normal mode.

"I won't be surprised if this has something to do with the big tournament," Joe commented. "There's a lot of money wrapped up in the popular games, both for the game makers and the players. I hope you aren't pushing yourself too hard practicing with your friends. I hardly see you before dinner these days."

"Don't worry. I only play one full game of Nova a day. Most of the time we just fool around with pre-programmed maneuvers and learning the physics engine. The Stryx say it's a great educational tool."

"Paul, I want to ask you something." Joe's tone became uncharacteristically sober, leading the boy to rise and stand awkwardly in anticipation of an embarrassing question. "All of these war games you play, you're not planning on becoming a mercenary in a few years, are you?"

"Do you think I'm crazy?" The boy exhaled in relief that it wasn't something serious. "I saw enough of that life before I was ten. But if I could turn pro at Nova and make some money, that would be cool. Maybe I'll buy you a new tug," he added with a grin.

"All right, I just wanted to ask. Hey, don't forget to give the consulate the ceiling coordinates for this patch." Joe squinted against the lights to read the numbers and letters. "It looks like N5045 by E732."

"I make it N8048 by E132," Paul corrected him. "When's the last time you had your eyes checked?"

"At my last fitness board," Joe replied. "Let's see, that was, oh, four years ago?"

"It's a good thing you don't have to shoot stuff for a living anymore," the boy teased Joe. "It's not like an eye test is a visit to the dentist. Anyway, I'll see you later."

"Not if I see you first," Joe retorted.

"Yeah, that's really likely," Paul answered with a laugh. "And if you do stop and get your eyes checked, don't use your implants to magnify the charts. That defeats the whole purpose."

Ten

After the last two dates, Kelly was beginning to think of her black cocktail dress as a suit of armor to don before combat. She decided to wear her hair up for a change, since she was sure there would be no difficulty in connecting with a man who was wearing yellow pants. Did some evil ex-girlfriend tell him that the pants matched his hair? They were meeting at the People Bowl, in the high rent section of the Little Apple, and she was looking forward to seeing how the other half lived.

Kelly arrived just a little early and entered the People Bowl through a spooky tunnel that glowed with soft blue light. Her date was already waiting for her, yellow pants and all. He approached with a confident stride and produced a dozen roses from behind his back, like a conjuring trick.

"Thanks, I think I know these roses," she said, and then accepted them graciously. "I'm Kelly, and you are?"

"Sangrid Khan," he replied, and indicated their table. "I can't tell you how much I've been looking forward to our date."

"That's so sweet of you." Kelly favored him with a warm smile, after which he shocked her by pulling out her chair to make it easier for her to take her place in the cramped restaurant. All of the restaurants and cafes on the station featured sardine tin seating due to the space

85

constraints, but the People Bowl took crowding to a new level. A good third of the floor space was taken up with the broad base of a glass dome filled with a translucent blue gas. As soon as she adjusted to the light, Kelly noticed that there were some darker blue stains floating within the gas, which circulated with an unseen current.

"Looks like the filter system for their fancy lighting is clogging up," Kelly ventured to break the ice, while Sangrid studied the menu like it was a prop in a play. "Still, it's a neat idea. I've never seen anything like it."

"Ah, so this is your first time here. Those are Harrians floating about in the plasma. The gas is tetrafluoromethane, I believe."

"Alright, never mind the tetrafloor-whatever, let's focus on the Harrians. Are they animal, mineral or vegetable?"

"Hmm, I don't think they fall into any of those categories, but they are definitely sentient. They pay to come and watch us eat. Apparently they find it refreshing, but only people with excellent vision can pick them out," Sangrid explained, completing his perusal of the menu and setting it aside. "The pasta is very good here, and all of the salad ingredients are fresh from the ag decks. Do you have any special dietary constraints, or would you like me to order for you?"

"You can order, thanks. I eat pretty much everything," Kelly replied.

"Omnivorous with stable digestion, that's very good," he praised her. "No food allergies that you're aware of?"

"No, none at all," Kelly replied with a grin. "My family tree looks like a forest. I have that hybrid vigor."

"And a healthy immune system, I'll bet," Sangrid said approvingly. He tapped on the menu icons to place their order. "I thought a bottle of wine would be nice as well. I hope you don't have any problems with alcohol?"

"No, no," Kelly replied, and took up the game. "I know some people believe that redheads can't handle their booze, but I assure you it's an old wives tale."

"I knew that color was natural!" Sangrid practically beamed. "I'll bet that those perfect teeth you flashed earlier are your own as well."

"I do what I can," Kelly said. She laughed outright at the direction of the conversation. If he thought she wouldn't sit there all night accepting compliments, he was going to find out just how wrong he was.

"I must apologize in advance for the service being a bit slow here," Sangrid told her, while he fished inside his dinner jacket and pulled out a red velvet sack. "I brought along a little game to help pass the time." He poured the contents of the bag onto the table and picked out a wooden block with symbols on the sides. Suddenly, he tossed it to her with a flick of his thumb, saying, "Have you ever seen one of these?"

Kelly's hand shot up and she caught the game piece right in front of her nose. This feat surprised her so much that she decided to play it cool and not say anything about the appropriateness of flinging something at your date's face without warning.

"I think I've seen my friend's daughters playing this game. Something to do with taking turns building a tower?" she guessed.

"Excellent. That's exactly it," he said, bobbing his head approvingly. "The trick is, you have to stack them with the surface glyphs matching, but you can't cover more than two of the red dots on the outline of the glyph at any point."

"Oh, I see." Kelly did a quick survey of the game pieces out on the table. "Do we get to pick them from the pile, or do we pick blindly from the bag?"

"I'm beginning to think you're hustling me," he joked, looking more pleased by the minute. "Dropsie can be played open face or closed face. The gamblers play closed face, of course."

"Shall I just start then?" Kelly asked. She carefully balanced the piece he'd thrown at her on top of a block on the table, positioning its glyph against the identical glyph, leaving two dots exposed.

"Ah, I won't give you such an easy one." He grinned wickedly and stacked a matching block over her play, so that almost half of its weight was hanging over the edge in thin air.

"Cruel, cruel," Kelly protested, studying the faces of the blocks for options. Then she made her choice and balanced the block gently on the stack, bringing the mass of the whole back towards the center.

"Perfect, not a hint of a tremor," Sangrid proclaimed, then suddenly swept the little tower and the remaining blocks back into the bag. "Wine's here."

"You certainly keep things moving right along," Kelly observed. A waiter poured wine into their glasses, and then paused to give them a chance to approve of the vintage.

"Thank you. I'm sure it's fine." Sangrid spoke brusquely to chase away the waiter. "I propose a toast," he continued, raising his glass so high that the bottom of his face was concealed as he whispered, "Can you hear me now?"

"Yes." Kelly laughed, and then she narrowed her eyes conspiratorially and whispered in an even lower register, "Can you hear me now?"

"Very good, very good." Sangrid took a long sip of wine, and when he set the glass back on the table his smile grew broader than ever. Without the slightest show of self-consciousness, he placed his right elbow on the table, the hand open, and then he laid his left forearm on the table so the left hand was directly below the right. "Arm wrestle?"

Uh oh. The warning bells went off in Kelly's head. This had just moved from a little eccentric to very weird. But he looked happy and, well, normal, so she hated to decline. Who knows? Maybe he spent the last few years in some place where this was acceptable behavior. She forced a chuckle, crossed palms with his right hand, and grasped the left on the table.

"Go," he said. Kelly reflexively tried to push his hand down, but she could tell he was only pushing back hard enough to keep their arms vertical, not trying to beat her. That was a little insulting, so she shifted her weight on the chair and tried harder, putting her shoulder into it. He looked a little surprised as his arm was forced backwards, but also happy, and then he exerted himself more strongly and forced her arm back to the vertical. Kelly made another effort, which met with the same result, and then she slacked off and he released both of her hands.

"Great, just great," Sangrid enthused, as if he was a physical trainer helping her to rehab from an injury. "Quick reactions, nice balance of fast twitch and slow twitch muscles. You really exceed all expectations, Kelly."

"Thank you, Sangrid, but I'm beginning to have a strange feeling about all of this." She kept her tone light, but there was no mistaking that she wasn't entirely comfortable with the way the date was going. "I've never been on a job interview, but I imagine it would be something like this."

"You've hit the nail right on the head," he confirmed her guess, and slapped his hand on the table. "You have an excellent grasp of analogies and pattern recognition."

Kelly felt herself starting to blush on hearing the high points of her self-image acknowledged and played back by a stranger, but she had no path other than forward. "So you see our date as a job interview?" she asked hesitantly, as the worm of doubt burrowed into the positive impression she had started to form of this cheerful, if somewhat peculiar man.

"Why, of course courting is like a job interview," he replied, sounding almost surprised. "What could be more important than picking the right person to contribute half of the genes to your offspring? And would you want to accidentally fall in love with somebody you wouldn't have chosen as a partner in a business?"

"You make the whole thing sound like a business," Kelly complained. "Don't you want romance, mutual attraction, that special spark?"

"We're neither of us children, Kelly," he remonstrated her, the beginnings of a frown appearing on his jovial countenance. "When people are well-matched, love may follow. But even if it doesn't, they're still well-matched, aren't they?"

Kelly opened her mouth to reply and then closed it. She wasn't going to debate him on the merits of love matches on a first date, but something about his vibe didn't exactly match his words.

"It seems to me that well-matched needs to go beyond physical characteristics," Kelly said slowly. "I get the feeling that you're more focused on the offspring side of the issue."

"Amazing, perfect, you really read my mind, Kelly," he said, recovering his good humor. "That's exactly what I wanted to talk about, but I couldn't quite see how to bring it up. You see, I would be perfectly willing to pay you to have my child. I wouldn't even insist on natural conception, as attractive as that proposition appears." He concluded this speech with a charming smile, as if she should receive his proposition as the ultimate compliment.

Kelly slumped in her chair for a moment, and then she pushed back from the table and rose to her feet. "I really don't have anything else to say to you Sangrid. Thank you for the wine."

"Wait, wait," he objected frantically, reaching across the table and grabbing her wrist. "Just hear me out. If it's pregnancy that scares you, we could arrange for a host mother. I would pay you for your eggs."

She regarded him in horror, made more acute by the dawning fear that Eemas had set her up with this guy because their profiles matched. Sangrid mistook her momentary paralysis for second thoughts, and continued with his pitch.

"I can't offer top dollar of course. You'll have to admit you're a couple of years past prime for egg harvesting, but I guarantee it will be worth your while," he pleaded.

Kelly jerked her wrist away, fixed him with a fierce stare, then grabbed the roses and rushed blindly from the restaurant. From aliens, to bride-stealers, to this jerk. Was it possible that her options were really this bad? Finding her way to the main drag of the Little Apple, she spotted Blythe working the outside tables of a café.

"Flowers for the lady, sir," she heard Blythe's practiced patter. "Buy a flower from a poor girl, Missus." Kelly caught her eye and motioned her to come over.

"How's business?" Kelly asked the girl, unable to suppress a grin at the begrimed face and the shabby dress.

"Great, Aunty Kelly," Blythe answered. "I've only got these left, and Chastity ran out a while ago. It's a big date night."

"Do you want to buy these?" Kelly proffered the dozen roses she'd received from Sangrid.

Blythe bit her lower lip, and then glancing around as if she was worried somebody could be paying attention, she led Kelly into the doorway of a clothing store that was closed for the evening.

"We don't really accept returns, Aunty Kelly, but since it's you, I could go 10 centees," she offered. "That's almost what we pay the wholesaler for new, and yours are used."

"You really are good at this, aren't you?" Kelly grimaced and handed over the roses. "Are you girls saving up for anything special?"

"Can you keep a secret?" Blythe whispered, her eyes shiny with excitement.

"That depends, Blythe. If I thought you were going to do something that impacted your family, I guess I'd have to tell your mother."

"Well, never mind then," Blythe replied shortly. "If you'll excuse me, I have flowers to sell."

"Hey, what about my 10 centees?" Kelly protested.

"Oh, see Chastity about that. She handles the accounts payable," Blythe replied matter-of-factly before starting back in on her pitch. "Fresh roses, 25 centees a dozen."

Kelly started after her, then turned and headed off in the other direction, towards the Burger Bar. She had just enough money to treat herself to a normal dinner, one without voyeuristic plasma creatures watching her chew. It was probably bad for karma to sell date flowers in any case, no matter how rotten the date.

Eleven

Joe dispensed with the silver suit for his second Eemas date in the theory that it had brought him bad luck. Instead he wore an old dress uniform with all the identifying marks removed. The buttons were a little tight across his gut, but sorting through metal scrap helped keep him in shape, especially since mass doesn't disappear with weight in lower gravity and his tendency was to just lift more. Chasing Beowulf around the scrap yard to get back his gloves helped also, though he couldn't get over the feeling that the dog was exercising him like a four-legged drill sergeant.

The date was at Camelot, a medieval-themed hotel casino that was primarily popular with humanoid species who favored edged weapons. Most sentient beings who retained personal weaponry ended up eschewing the advanced hand weapons that could slice a building in half in favor of sharp and pointy things that cut and stabbed. You never knew if the other party would have defensive technology in place that could turn your energy or projectile weapons against you.

Hereditary rulers preferred not to have a lot of high-tech weapons that could turn every peasant into an army rattling around a planet. Sticking with old-fashioned weapons on the ground meant that trained soldiers had a tremendous advantage over rabbles and militias, but as soon as spaceships were involved, victory went to the technically advanced. Most interplanetary and interspecies conflicts were fought and decided with words, before any large-scale bloodshed took place.

Joe's dress uniform was really a standard officer's uniform that didn't have any repair patches on it, patches which frequently aligned with scars on his skin. It was primarily recognizable as a military uniform by the number of pockets and loops for holding various weapons and other field necessities. Stripped of combat survival gear, it resembled something an upscale tradesman might wear.

As he cut through the Little Apple on his way to Camelot, wearing the uniform brought Joe's senses onto high alert, and he spotted an ambush laid by the flower girl in time to cross to the other side of the main drag. Chuckling to himself, he looked back over his shoulder to see how she reacted to being outsmarted, and then came to a dead stop as something soft bounced off of his long legs. A tearful little face looked up at him.

"Please excuse me," Joe stammered, finding he had almost run down a petite ten-year-old girl in an old frock with smudges on her face.

"Oh, sir, look what you've done to my flowers." The girl stared up at him pathetically while pointing at the mound of yellow daisies on the walkway. Joe was no horticultural expert, but they looked slightly wilted to him, perhaps leftovers from a slow evening the night before. But he knew when he was beat.

"How much for the lot?" he asked, trying to sound cheerful about it.

"All of them?" Her eyes opened so wide that they seemed to stretch from one side of her head to the other, with just the thinnest strip of nose to keep them apart. "We usually get 15 centees a dozen for daisies, but since you're taking all of them, I could make you a special price of 50 centees for the lot." Without waiting for an answer, she squatted down and rapidly aligned the stems of the fallen flowers into a bulging bouquet, which to Joe's eye, looked like it contained less than three dozen daisies. He sighed and fished a handful of coins out of his pocket.

"Are you related to the girl selling flowers across the corridor?" he asked to cover his embarrassment, separating out two 25-centee pieces for her.

"She's my older sister," the girl replied, taking the money. "We're saving to buy a baby brother."

"Is buying a baby brother legal?" Joe asked in surprise, not being all that well informed about family law on the station.

"Of course," the girl told him, with a look that suggested he had just arrived from some backwards mining colony with no running water. "The Stryx always balance their books."

"What does that have to do with it?" Joe was genuinely curious to figure out what was behind the flower mafia, but then he remembered that he was on his way to a date. "I wish you and your sister luck with the baby brother thing."

"Thank you, sir." The girl bobbed her head and dropped a cute curtsey that took the sting out of the transaction.

Five minutes later, Joe strode into the Camelot with his monster bouquet of flowers, wondering if he should have just picked out the nicest daisy and thrown the rest into a disposal chute. He was ashamed to admit, even to himself, that the only thing stopping him from doing so was the suspicion that one of those little girls would pop out from nowhere and catch him in the act. Joe wasn't sure if he was more afraid that their feelings would be hurt or that they would sell him a new batch.

The notification from Eemas had described his date as "regal, blue veil, silver spurs," so Joe assumed she would be easy to spot. Looking around the faux stone hall with the giant artificial fireplace, fake torches in sconces, and the dinging of slot machines in the distance, he was struck by the number of blue veiled damsels jangling about in silver spurs. As he stood trying to decide his next move, a particularly regal figure separated herself from the mob and approached him.

"Welcome, our hero," she spoke regally, extending her arm with the hand hanging palm downwards. Joe had fought on enough feudalisticly governed worlds to guess that she expected him to take her hand and either drop to one knee or bend deeply at the waist and brush her knuckles with a kiss. He went with the second option, and after releasing her hand, extended the overstuffed bouquet.

"Joe McAllister, at your service," he introduced himself. "I'm glad you were able to spot me from my description. I didn't expect to see so many blue veiled women wearing spurs."

"But we are the only queen here! Queen Ayre, you may address us," she said imperiously. "Surely you were looking directly at us before we approached, as befitting the lady of the castle in greeting a suitor."

"Uh, yes, of course," Joe answered, trying to deconstruct the implant's interpretation of a speech pattern which he had the nagging feeling he had heard in the past. On impulse, he triggered the mental switch to put the implant on hold, and waited for her to begin speaking again.

"We can see by these flowers that you have journeyed a long way over a difficult path," she continued, with just a hint of regal sarcasm. "Let us remove to the dining hall where a repast awaits hungry travelers."

Vergallian! The language came back to him in an instant, and he silently thanked his deceased mother who had opened his mind to the love of learning languages in his childhood. Joe had spent over six years in Vergallian space, and as he followed Queen Ayre to the dining hall, he wracked his memory for details about their culture.

The Vergallians dominated a large number of star systems with a strange mix of feudal society and advanced technology. A general on Hwoult Five once mentioned to Joe in passing that an invasion fleet was being prepared to add Earth to the Empire of a Hundred Worlds at the time the Stryx stepped in and took the humans under their protection. While the Vergallians were not pleased with the interference, neither did they consider Earth any great loss.

Silver spurs jingling, she led him into a narrow dining hall with a long table running down the center. Minstrels near the entrance plucked at crude stringed instruments, which had the beneficial effect of softening the casino noises into what could have been expected from a distant street carnival or a joust. Queen Ayre halted next to an empty spot at the table, and Joe moved quickly to pull out a chair, into which she settled with regal grace. He took the seat at her right, which he now recalled was the assigned place for a fighting man. The left-hand seat was traditionally saved for the wise man or the fool, but he couldn't recall which.

"We are pleased to find a well-bred knight so far from home," Queen Ayre said, turning to him. She lifted her veil and threw it back over her hair, revealing the chiseled, symmetrical features typical of the Vergallian elite. "Are you familiar with our lovely domains?"

"Can't say that I am," Joe replied in English, since speaking Vergallian would put lie to his words. She did specify "our" domains, he reflected, and Joe had never heard her name before. An inkling of a half-remembered rumor made him play his cards close to the vest. The Vergallians hadn't amassed an empire without chewing up and spitting out the unwary. "Is this your first Eemas date?"

Queen Ayre lost her regal bearing for a split second, and behind the mask of her exquisitely formed features flashed a look of irritation. "Nooo," she drawled slowly, taking a moment to formulate a reply. "We have not been pleased with the heroes selected by Eemas to this point. We have very high standards."

"I see." Joe nodded his acknowledgement to the waiter or serving man, who placed two mugs of foaming ale before them. "Well, what are you doing so far from home?"

"We are seeking a hero," she proclaimed, recovering her poise and fixing him with a hypnotic stare. Joe began to feel highly vulnerable as he remembered that some Vergallian women could produce human compatible pheromones that would put a queen bee to shame. "Are you a hero, Joe?"

"Well, I'm still alive, so if I am a hero, I must be pretty good at it." Joe took a sip of the ale, and then he set down his mug and attempted a roguish smile, the impact of which was blunted by the heavy foam sticking to his upper lip.

"Are you afraid of death, Joe?" she asked, watching him intently. "Would you not gamble all to win a kingdom and a lady fair?"

"I might at that," Joe answered, intending it as a compliment to her beauty rather than as a commitment. Her smile hit him like a flash grenade, and the afterimage made him wonder if he'd actually been strobed by a mini-blinder. After a couple of blinks his vision cleared, just in time to see her stowing away a small blue vial in her boot.

"You have led cavalry in war, yes? We detected signs in your walk and the way you hold yourself that you are at home in the saddle."

"It's been a few years since I worked as a horse soldier," he admitted, taking another sip of the ale. It seemed to have gone flat already, or maybe ale brewed to an authentic old recipe changed flavor and lost fizz rapidly after it was drawn from the barrel. Joe also began to wonder if the pheromones were getting at him, since he suddenly felt hazy. He took another pull at the ale in hopes it would clear his head.

"In these wars where you led cavalry, did you win?" she pressed on. Somehow, coming up with the answer she wanted to hear took on a sudden urgency. But if there was one thing Joe couldn't lie about, it was fighting.

"Won some, lost some, never got killed," he mumbled, thick-tongued. "Hey, how about we go somewhere a little quieter and I'll show you my scars?" He flubbed an attempt to stand up because both of his legs felt like they were falling asleep. The pins-and-needles sensation in his left leg included a pain more reminiscent of a dagger stick. "What 'zactly are you offering, lady Queen?"

"Ourselves!" she spoke proudly, striking a regal pose in her chair. "The Vergallian Cycle is coming to completion on Terwell, and we require an off-world hero to retain for us our rightful inheritance."

Vergallian Cycle, Joe repeated to himself. Wasn't that the reason he had been fighting on Hwoult Five, a battle for succession that took place according to some astrological schedule? There was something about it that he just couldn't quite put his finger on, but what was it? Something related to immolation? He reactivated the translation implant in hopes it would do a better job with the details.

"Only once every thirty-two years is the competition for supremacy on Terwell open to outsiders. We requested Eemas to find us a hero with the courage and experience to lead a unit of cavalry in the competition for our hand in matrimony," she continued, and each word seemed to drive a warm spike through his heart. Yes, here was a woman to fight for, to wager one's life against a kingdom.

"Yes," he said out loud, barely aware of the fact he had spoken. Queen Ayre whipped a parchment scroll tied with an ornate silken ribbon from her sleeve, and she rapidly unrolled and smoothed the somewhat stained and abused document before him on the table. Next she pulled a messy inkpot from a hidden pocket, followed by a wicked looking quill.

"Just sign here at the bottom," she instructed him, priming the quill with red ink and forcing it into his hand. "Sign, and it's off to the honeymoon suite, where we will open a world of pleasures to our hero."

"Just sign," he repeated thickly. His eyes tried to focus on the proper area of the parchment and he struggled to read the calligraphed letters from an alphabet he hadn't seen in years. "Where it says, 'Sacrificial King?'"

Queen Ayre's face went white with rage. She snatched back the scroll and rapidly rolled it up into a tight baton. Joe swayed in his chair, unclear what he could have done to upset the most desirable woman he'd ever met in his life. Then he slumped forward onto the table and passed out. Nobody took any notice as the Queen rose, replaced her veil, and swept regally from the room.

The effects of the drugged ale wore off in less than a half hour, which gave the pheromone-induced clouds time to clear from Joe's head as well. When he came to, he had to peel the side of his face from the table, where a previous customer had spilled mead and oatmeal. The moment he levered himself back into an upright position, a serving man carrying a nasty looking mace appeared with the check.

"That's two Galahad Ales at 1 cred, plus 50 centees for sleeping on the table and a 25 centee suggested gratuity," the serving man recited, twirling a heavy mace idly by the wrist loop.

"I wasn't finished with my ale," Joe protested out of pride, but he knew he hadn't recovered sufficiently from whatever had happened to take on the tavern enforcer.

"I think you've had quite enough, sir," the serving man replied dryly.

Joe mulled that over for a long moment and decided the serving man's assessment was accurate, even if was based on a misreading of the situation. So he reached in his pocket without rising from his seat and fished out a handful of bloody coins.

"Allow me, sir." Setting aside his mace, the man produced a finger bowl, filled it with water from a carafe on the table, and indicated that Joe should drop in his bloody coins. The serving man swirled the water around the bowl a few times like a prospector panning for gold, then expertly poured most of the pink liquid off onto the floor without losing a centee.

Watching this operation reminded Joe that the bloody coins had come from his clean dress uniform pocket, and looking down, he found that the leather over his left thigh was crusted over with dried blood. A small cut which looked suspiciously like a prick from a lady's dagger or a sharp quill went right through the pocket. So that's where red ink comes from, Joe thought sourly. He wasn't happy that his only flawless uniform had been bloodied on a date, of all things.

When he looked up again, the serving man bowed deeply and intoned, "That was very generous of you, sir." Then the man retreated, leaving the bowl with a few small denomination coins on the table.

Twelve

"I'm not bailing out on the subscription," Kelly told Donna, trying not to sound like she was asking permission. "But it would look pretty odd if I didn't show up for the first embassy-sponsored mixer, which, if I may add, was my idea."

"Why didn't you just put in a change request to Eemas for a date to meet you there?" Donna asked skeptically.

"Maybe my decade and a half of experience doesn't make me a singles expert, but I know you don't bring a date to a mixer."

"So you could have pretended that you met by chance."

"Do I really look so pathetic that I need to arrange a back-up date for a mixer?" Kelly asked. "Anyway, it's too late now, and based on the dates I've been on when Eemas had weeks to think about it, I don't want to see who I would get on one hour's notice after a cancellation."

"Well, you can explain it to the girls when they ask how your date went. They've been nagging me about getting them a baby brother lately, and I had to explain that it wasn't as simple as just ordering one from a catalog." Donna looked away guiltily and added, "So, uh, don't be surprised if they start in on you about having a baby."

"Donna!"

"Well, you're not getting any younger, and you did have an offer, even if it was a little creepy."

104

"A little creepy? That man wanted to pay me to have a baby for HIM, or barring that, to sell him my eggs!"

"I have to go make dinner for the girls," Donna said, choosing not to extend the conversation. "I'll see you at the mixer. If it doesn't work out, you can help me with the nametags and the messaging list, but I won't be able to get you overtime pay."

"You get paid overtime?" Kelly asked in dismay.

"Of course, I'm hourly." Donna sounded exasperated with her friend's thick-headedness as she rushed for the door. "See you."

Kelly decided against returning home for another shower before the mixer, in part because her morning ablutions had become an experience in terror as the landlord program turned downright nasty. If Mr. Right showed up for the mixer, he'd have to take Kelly as she was. Besides, duty called.

"Libby? Do you have anything new on those invasive black vines that were discovered growing on the open ag deck? The farmer denied all knowledge, and he was afraid to touch the stuff himself so he's asked the embassy for help."

A short pause ensued, enough to make Kelly wonder if Libby wasn't listening, but as usual, the Stryx hadn't missed a word.

"We ran tests on samples and it's been positively identified as a new strain of Blanker, which is banned in Stryx space. Maintenance bots have eradicated the vines and are in the process of inspecting the ground level on all of the ag decks," Libby reported.

"What exactly is Blanker?"

"It's a bio-engineered mind altering drug," Libby explained. "I don't believe you've encountered any of the

Farlings in your travels, but they are one of the most technologically advanced biologicals in this part of the galaxy, especially in genetic engineering. A few of the outer Farling systems are connected to our tunnel network, but most Farling worlds are beyond our influence. They are not aggressive themselves, but they have been known to provide advanced technology to other biologicals. In short, Blanker gives the user a false sense of confidence, of being in complete control of the situation, while simultaneously slowing reaction times by a few percent."

"What's so horrible about that?" Kelly asked. "Does it have long term effects, or do the users build up resistance and need to buy more and more of the stuff?"

"No. It's specifically designed to be non-addictive and nearly undetectable, so it can be introduced into food supplies for a whole community without being discovered."

"Then I really don't get it. There are humans all over the galaxy addicted to substances that destroy their minds and their bodies. To buy another dose, they'll steal from their parents or sell their children into slavery. Who would care about a drug that makes people a little overconfident while slowing them down just a hair?"

Then Kelly's analytical side took over, and without waiting for Libby to reply, she began thinking it through out loud.

"If there was a war on and you could get it into enemy supplies, but no, they'd be testing for that. It sounds like it could shift the odds a little in a sporting event, help the gamblers against the spread, but there aren't any professional Earth leagues on this side of the galaxy. The only humans around here I can imagine having a problem with Blanker are the competitive gamers," she concluded.

"Exactly," Libby confirmed her hypothesis. "From Phalnyx to blitz chess, from Nova to Artellian poker, the one thing humanity excels at is playing games. The Natural League is founded on the premise that the biologicals who developed space travel without Stryx intervention are superior in every way to the species we've fostered. But you humans have an unexpected knack for games, and I'm sure you're aware that the rise of human champions at competitive tournaments has boosted Earth's game exports by several orders of magnitude. Outside of Stryx space, the most common cause of shooting wars is market share."

"I guess I'll have to take your word for that," Kelly replied. "So you're suggesting a conspiracy between alien game manufacturers and Natural League members with fragile egos to cheat at the Union Station tourney?"

"The probability is in excess of 99.94%," Libby answered modestly.

"Why does the universe have to be so weird?" Kelly complained. But then again, it made perfect sense, in an alien sort of a way.

"Speaking of our weird universe, I hear that somebody cancelled on her dream date tonight."

"Why don't you just admit that you run Eemas. I promise I won't tell anybody."

"Alright, I run Eemas, and I had you set up with the perfect match tonight. Why did you cancel?" Libby sounded genuinely annoyed.

"Libby, I may not be a maestro of relationships, but those first three guys you picked for me were the worst. I understand that compared to all of the other Eemas clients, working with humans is new to you, but I'm beginning to wonder if you just don't get us. I mean, what kind of success rate do you have with humans compared to everybody else?"

"You've got a point there," Libby admitted, and Kelly could almost hear the smile in the Stryx's synthesized voice. "Before I extended the Eemas service to humans, the success rate was so close to perfect that publishing a percentage didn't even make sense. Humans have single-handedly dragged down my success rate by almost a full point, which means over half of my attempts at human matchmaking are failing. I've issued more refunds in the last two decades than in the previous millennia."

"So why do you keep promoting the service to humans?"

"For one thing, it's a business, and for another, I like a challenge. At this point, I'm mainly using the dates to learn more about human relationships. Do you want to hear my conclusions?"

"Uh, okay," Kelly replied, not really sure that this was a good idea, but unwilling to try to explain her discomfort to Libby.

"Uniquely among the biologicals, large numbers of humans either don't know what they want, or they lie to themselves about what they do want. It's why your immersives and literature do so poorly in translation. To use your own words, the rest of the galaxy just doesn't 'get' humans. Your development as a species depends on natural selection, yet your mating selections are most unnatural."

"Is that why you don't provide pictures or videos before the dates, just the vague physical description? You think we're too picky or something?"

"No, I like to leave the door open to chance. The important thing when you go on a blind date is that you're open to meeting somebody new. Maybe you'll mistakenly meet the wrong person but it's simply meant to be. I often schedule multiple Eemas introductions for the same location at the same time, just to give nature a chance."

"Doesn't sound very omniscient to me," Kelly objected.

"Humans are tough to quantify. At the risk of sounding egotistical, I'm afraid the fault lies with human inconsistency, not my analytical ability. So if I may ask again, why did you cancel your date?"

"Oh, that's just because the embassy is sponsoring a singles mixer," Kelly replied, but she was no longer sure that it was true.

"I see," Libby responded after an artificially long pause, confirming Kelly's suspicions that the Stryx didn't believe the acting ambassador knew her own mind.

"Anyway, I don't believe my dates were really dates at all. You're just using me to catch bride-stealers or cancel contracts and the like."

"Or perhaps I concluded from your personal data that you needed preparation," Libby offered the alternative explanation. "Matchmaking isn't a simple service, it's a process. Maybe I'm just making sure that you'll be in the right state of mind to accept Mr. Right when I drop him in your lap."

"I've got to get going or I'll be too late to meet anyone." Kelly rose abruptly and headed for the corridor. Then a flash of bravado led her to add, "I'll let you know tomorrow whether or not you can cancel my remaining introductions."

"I think I'm safe there," Libby responded dryly, and withdrew from contact.

Thirteen

The opposing battle fleets scrambled and unscrambled themselves in the intricate ballet that preceded a full-scale commitment to total war. Paul controlled the blue fleet, Joe the red, and although they sat just an arm's length apart over the glowing Nova cube with its holographic projections, they were barely aware of each other's presence. The game was famous for its intensity, and even combat veterans of multiple fleet actions, like Joe, were liable to break into a cold sweat just skirmishing over the initial dispositions. Beowulf sat by the man's side, occasionally whining softly or scratching the floor plates when he didn't agree with Joe's choices.

A full game of Nova lasted on the order of four hours, although the exact timing depended on how long it took the host star to explode, which was a random element in the game. The fleets were evenly matched in size and strength, an artificiality never encountered in the real world, which meant that victory went to the player with the best battle management abilities. A blast of X-rays released from the star teetering on the edge of self-destruction signaled the start of the game.

"Damn!" Joe muttered, as tiny flashes in the left wing of his formation witnessed the compromise of his starting position. "Aren't you even going to let me compete, boy?"

Paul didn't answer, intent on the holo-gesture controller on his side of the Nova cube. Practiced finger movements allowed him to maneuver and fight the squadrons, even individual ships within a squadron, a level of control that Joe could only marvel at. He ground his teeth and executed one of his previously programmed fallback plans, bringing the right wing and high squadrons to cover the retreat of the left, and placing his forces in a defensive hedgehog formation.

With the boy already ahead on ships, Joe knew he would have to transition to the offensive at some point before the star went nova and Paul won on points. He moved his hands within the controller space and dripped beads of sweat as Beowulf whined louder and nipped at his arm. It was beginning to look like he could lose his fleet before the star even popped, the ultimate humiliation for a Nova player. It was time to get serious.

"What do you know about girls?" Joe managed to ask in a casual tone, even as one of his tunnel projectors took a direct hit. "I've been thinking it's time we had a little talk."

"Don't bother, Joe." Paul didn't miss a beat as his ships attacked and swirled around the ex-mercenary's staggering formations. "The Stryx school covered all that stuff in the biologicals survey last year, and they say we have pretty outlandish mating habits. Speaking of which, what happened to your big date tonight?"

Beowulf barked frantically and gestured at the incoming flare with his nose. Joe's forces were hemmed in, and the hot plasma from the star tore through his reserves like water from a dam bursting above a matchstick boat race.

"Triggering a flare is cheating," Joe griped, even though he knew that it was within the rules if you had the ability to pull it off. What it meant was that Paul had been decimating Joe's fleet with just a fraction of his own forces as the rest concentrated their weapons on the star's photosphere to create instability. Joe had been so busy defending he'd never even seen it. But now, with his operational forces shrunk to half of their original strength, he was more comfortable maneuvering and chose to beat a strategic retreat. His best hope now was that the induced flare would speed up the nova clock. Beowulf shook his giant head and curled up to go to sleep.

"Sorry, Joe," Paul apologized, easing up on his attack pressure. "I've been waiting to try that against somebody good. I passed the final qualifiers for the station tourney, and there are going to be some Natural League grandmasters there. I just don't want to look bad."

"Alright," Joe grumbled. "Then I'm glad I could be of service. But I'd been hoping to fill in some time this evening after my date cancelled, and it's been what, fifteen minutes?"

"Are you trying to get married, Joe?" The ships in the Nova cube sorted themselves back into distinct colored masses as the opposing forces regrouped.

"Well, I've never had a chance to put down roots. This junkyard is the first home I've had since I was a kid. I was thinking it might be nice to give it a shot, being a real family and all."

"Is it my fault you aren't married yet?" The boy lifted his eyes up from the game for the first time, looking both younger and more vulnerable than Joe had seen him in some time.

"Yes," Joe answered, and then took advantage of Paul's momentary shock to trigger his pre-programmed last stand. A haze of flashes filled the Nova cube as suicidal attackers struck home, and they wreaked havoc among the boy's recently reformed battle groups before he could recover. Conversation over, the two players became reabsorbed in the game and fought it out for another half an hour before the star ripped itself apart prematurely. Paul still won the game handily on points, but Joe felt that he'd achieved a moral victory.

"Never take your mind off the game, kiddo," Joe crowed to the boy. "Oldest trick in the book."

Beowulf came out of his nap with a soft growl and lifted his head, tilting an ear towards the entrance of Mac's Bones. But after an elaborate stretching routine, he clunked back down on his rug and returned to his dreams.

"It's Jeeves," Paul reported. "He was coming by for a game tonight, but I told him to hold off after you ended up staying home. I just let him know we finished, so I guess he was in the area."

"He was in the area because you didn't expect me to last this long," Joe grumbled. But he was proud that the boy could beat him easily at most games, and he could always claim the credit of having been Paul's first teacher. "Who's this Jeeves? I don't remember hearing you mention him before."

"Oh, you've met him. He's the Stryx kid that went out on that tug job with you a few weeks ago, the one where you brought back that Sharf cabin cruiser. I ran into him at the gaming club after that, and we've been playing pretty regular since."

"He's a Stryx kid? I thought he was on the immature side. I guess that explains the attitude anyway." Joe grimaced, recalling the robot's continual put-downs. "First Stryx I ever met with a self-esteem problem."

"I didn't realize you were such an expert on Stryx." The robot's voice broke into the conversation, causing Joe to jump up and spin around. Jeeves floated soundlessly through the makeshift door into the improvised living room of the converted ice harvester, looking oddly naked without all the attachments he'd borne the last time Joe had seen him.

"Hey, Jeeves," Paul greeted the robot. "I tried that flare trick I've been developing. It worked great."

"Of course it did," Jeeves replied, leaving no doubt in Joe's mind that the Stryx was crediting Paul's success to weakness of his opponent, but the boy didn't seem to notice. "I believe there's enough time for us to play before you need to sleep."

"What are you going to spot the boy?" Joe asked, having better sense than to trade insults with an adolescent robot.

"We play straight up," Paul interjected, showing a rare flash of pride. "Jeeves always wins, of course, but I think I'm improving faster than he is."

"I've learned a great deal from playing Paul, which is especially remarkable given his early training." Jeeves addressed himself directly to Joe, who couldn't help wondering if all young Stryx had issues interacting with human adults. Maybe that's why they spent so much time playing with children, Joe thought, which gave rise to an idea.

"So, you'd say that playing against Paul has been valuable to you?" Joe inquired innocently.

"Very much so," Jeeves replied, in a show of youthful solidarity.

"And how have you been compensating him?"

"Hey, we're friends," Paul protested. "And whatever he says, I'm sure I'm learning more from him than he's learning from me!"

Jeeves pivoted from one human to the other while floating in place, like the needle of a compass dragged between headings by a magnet. The strict adherence of the Stryx to an honest barter economy was what enabled them to control so much of the galaxy without having to conquer by force. Everybody, even the species that hated the very idea of a non-biological intelligence, knew that the Stryx represented the best chance for a fair deal. The main opposition to the Stryx came from the empire-building cultures who couldn't risk attacking areas under Stryx protection, and the Natural League members, who resented what they saw as Stryx favoritism to backwards biologicals.

"The old one is correct," Jeeves said to Paul. "The games were my idea, and my own schooling is finished. I really should be providing something in return. Perhaps you'd like to move to more civilized quarters on a residential deck?"

"No, I'm fine here with Joe," Paul replied in embarrassment. "Never mind all that and let's get started."

"If you want to work off your obligation to the boy, I have a little job you can help with here," Joe spoke over Paul's protest. "I promise that the profits will go into fixing this place up so it will be less like living in a spaceship that happened to crash into a junkyard. Maybe I'll even hire some housekeeping help so Paul can stop eating sandwiches for every meal."

"May I enquire as to the substance of this little job?" Jeeves spoke in a careful tone that indicated a newfound respect for Joe's negotiating skills.

"Just helping me to identify some of the junk I've got lying around out there. Half the time I can't guess close enough what something might be to even start asking the station librarian questions about it," Joe admitted. "It's not the stuff I buy, but the junk that was here before I took over. Some of it could turn out to be dangerous for Paul, or even for the station. Like a gravitational vortex mine leftover from the Founding Wars."

"Vortex mines?" Jeeves sounded like he would have raised an eyebrow if he'd had eyebrows to lift. "Alright, you have a deal. Now run along to your date while we serious gamers get down to business."

"Date cancelled," Joe and Paul said simultaneously.

"It's a wonder they all don't cancel," Jeeves commented, and he began arranging his forces for the game.

Fourteen

The mixer was held in the Meteor room, one of the smaller ballrooms of the Empire Convention Center, which was popular with interstellar trade shows and academic conferences. Donna had logged just over a hundred preregistrations at two creds a head, which covered the room rental for two hours and included one free drink. Walk-ins were welcome for a 50-centee premium, and hopefully there would be enough to pay back the embassy's petty cash fund for the finger food provided by Empire catering.

It was really a Beta affair, and if it worked out, Donna planned to add a band at the next event, maybe open it to couples as well. The "classical" tracks pumped in softly over the room's sound system were only marginally better than the unidentifiable music that played in the tube capsules.

Kelly arrived late, found out that she had forgotten to preregister, and paid the premium for her nametag. Donna looked her up and down, obviously unimpressed that she had come straight from work without going home to change, but Kelly just mumbled "Long story," and entered the ballroom.

Once inside, she headed hopefully for the folding tables with the white tablecloths, but the party platters looked like they had been attacked by a flock of ravenous birds.

There were still plenty of crackers, but nothing remained of the dip, and the only slices of cheese left behind bore the telltale marks of having been sampled and rejected.

Then she spotted a discarded napkin formed like a crumpled canopy over the corner of a silver platter. With a sense of heightened anticipation, she grasped the peak between her thumb and forefinger and raised it slowly, while turning her head sideways to see what would be revealed. At the moment of truth, the torso of a blue-jacketed figure loomed into her vision.

"Hello. I'm Thomas. I arrived just after you."

"Hi Thomas, I'm Kelly." She straightened up, embarrassed, but unable to keep her eyes from straying back to the napkin and what it potentially concealed.

"I'm sorry, I think I interrupted you," Thomas apologized, with an exaggerated look of concern. He appeared to be a few years younger than Kelly, with medium length brown hair and no outstanding features that spoke for or against his looks. "Please continue what you were doing."

Kelly hesitated for a moment because the whole thing was so silly, getting caught hunting for a bit of finger food under a discarded napkin, and then turning away from a conversation to do so a second time. But she decided to take him at his word.

"Thanks, I'll just take a quick peek," she replied, and whipped off the napkin without any further ado. It revealed two slices of a spiraled bread roll that included some kind of white filling flecked with green olive. Synthesized tuna salad? Synthesized chicken salad? Her mouth began to water.

"Please, you have them both," Thomas encouraged her. "I don't need to eat things like that."

"Well, if you insist," Kelly agreed quickly, moving both rollups to a small plastic plate, and then taking a nibble of the first.

"They say the way to a woman's heart is through her stomach," Thomas ventured with a smile. His whole face rearranged itself around the upturned corners of his mouth and his strong, even teeth. Kelly immediately felt guilty.

"I think they usually say it about a man's heart and stomach," she admitted, and held out the plate. "It's very good. One is all I really wanted."

"A man's heart and stomach," Thomas repeated. "I believe you're right, but truly, I can't eat a bite."

"If you're sure?" Kelly smiled in relief, and made quick work of finishing the first rollup. Thomas stood quietly, observing, so she swallowed and asked, "Have you been on Union Station long?"

To her surprise, Thomas suddenly appeared to be acutely embarrassed. She watched him curiously as he shuffled his feet and looked around self-consciously. Finally, he came out with, "Actually, I'm not very good at dating."

An uncomfortable silence followed. Kelly chewed the second rollup and tried to come up with a polite way to lose the poor guy before the evening was shot. But then she spotted Donna looking skeptically in her direction, and she had the sudden urge to prove she could manage a date on her own. What could it hurt to give the shy guy another chance?

"So, do you happen to know anything about the Union Station gaming tourney?" Kelly asked. She hoped that the question would give Thomas an easy conversational entrée, and maybe provide her with some background information to help her understand the Blanker conspiracy that had just landed in her lap. "I'm supposed to attend the planning session as a diplomat, but I really know very little about it."

"I know a lot about the Union Station gaming tourney," Thomas replied, bursting with enthusiasm and renewed confidence. "Do you want to know about the history of the games, the events this cycle, the contestants, the prizes? I may be entered in one of the peripheral events myself if I qualify."

"Tell me about the contestants, Thomas. I'm especially interested in knowing about the competition in any games where humans will be competing for the championship."

"There are thirty-six events in the tourney, and humans can compete in seven of those. Of the seven, humans have a chance of winning five. The Drazens will win at Three Square until the rules are changed, because the endgame is a perfect match for their tentacle, and either the Frunge or Dollnicks will win at Trikado, because they can turn off their pain receptors and regenerate limbs later. But humans have a good chance at Phalnyx, Backgammon, Terror Drive, Foosball and Nova."

"Why can we only play in seven games?"

"Humans can't compete in games that require telekinetic ability, electromagnetic spectrum sensitivity beyond visible light, or other specialized biological functions that are lacking from human genetics. But winning five out of thirty-six would be a record. No species has ever taken more than three events since the tournament play was established."

"Do you know if humans will be facing champions from any of the Natural League worlds in those five events?" Kelly was starting to feel very pleased with herself for giving the guy a second chance and striking gold.

"There will be strong competition from Natural League worlds in everything but Foosball. The equipment cost and gravity requirements have prevented Foosball from catching on much outside of areas with a human presence, so it's primarily a mining colony game. The main competition will be from the Hortens, of course, since they traditionally own Phalnyx and excel at gambling games."

"Thank you very much, Thomas. That was extremely useful to me."

"I wish there was a real band," Thomas spoke wistfully. "I know how to dance very well."

"Really? It's surprising you're so shy in that case. My parents made us all learn how to dance when we were children and it's really come in handy for me as a diplomat. I think I could dance to this music, even though it sounds a little alien."

Thomas smiled happily and held out both arms in a perfect ballroom dancing pose. "So, shall we take a turn around the room while you tell me about working as a diplomat? It sounds very interesting."

Kelly stepped into his arms confidently, and they set off slowly around the room, occasionally dodging other waltzing couples. The waltz steps fit reasonably well with the piped-in alien music, which was composed in a triple meter. Two flower girls circled the milling adults like predatory wolves, expertly cutting out straggling couples and lightening their pockets in exchange for a sprig of violets.

Thomas proved to be an expert dancer and a confident lead, and Kelly found herself floating along as she recounted the triumphs and disasters of her diplomatic career. She couldn't remember anybody ever showing such an interest and asking such intelligent questions about her options and choices. Suddenly, it occurred to her that he might be a professional listener, a therapist of some sort. She was just about to ask him what he did for a living when the music stopped.

"Alright folks, I'm afraid our time is up," Donna's voice came over the PA system. "Thank you for attending. We hope you had as good a time as we did, and when I say you, I'm sure you know who I'm talking about. If you haven't signed up for our notification list, please stop and do so on your way out."

"Oh, can you believe how time flies?" Kelly asked Thomas, her green eyes sparkling. "How can two hours have gone by just like that? I'm afraid I've talked your ear off. I hope you'll let me make it up to you sometime."

"It couldn't have been two hours," Thomas replied, interpreting her statement literally. "Let's see. We arrived at the same time, and all of the food was gone, so we must have been late. Maybe we've only been here a few minutes?"

"Such a flatterer," Kelly said, laughing at his serious demeanor and giving him a nudge with her shoulder. "Oh, I really needed tonight, Thomas. Thank you." She looked quickly about to make sure they had a bit of privacy, and then she crossed her fingers and tried to prompt him into action. "Is there anything you wanted to ask me?"

"Yes, there is," Thomas exclaimed, his face breaking into the same wide smile she'd seen just once earlier. "Did I pass?"

"Of course you passed," Kelly said warmly, and chucked him on the shoulder. Still, she was a bit taken aback that his self-confidence could be so tenuous after the best evening of dancing she'd had in longer than she could remember. "Did you really have to ask?"

"Of course. I can't just declare myself to have passed the Turing/Ryskoff test. I'm hardly a disinterested judge," he explained. "Now I'll be able to present myself at the Tourney for Stryx certification and take my place among sentient beings. Are you alright, Kelly?" He grabbed the acting ambassador's elbows as she listed to the side on buckling knees. After a moment, she took a gasping breath and regained her balance, even though all of the color had drained from her face.

"You're an artificial person?" she whispered.

"Well, I prefer to be called Thomas, if you don't mind. I am a new artificial intelligence construct, conceived as a group project of the Open University Senior Class. There wasn't much of a budget, of course, so this body is a rental."

"Oh, Thomas. How could you," Kelly implored, fighting back tears for the first time in years. "I thought you were a human. How could an artificial person be so mean?"

"I don't understand," Thomas replied. His face took on a deep look of concern, which Kelly now realized was likely a preset expression from the rental company. "This is the Turing/Ryskoff open event sponsored by the remedial human program of the Open University. Didn't you attend the judging course?"

"No, Thomas, this is not the Turing/Ryskoff open event. This is the first social mixer sponsored by the EarthCent embassy on Union Station!"

"How can that be?" Thomas looked around, visibly upset. "The test was scheduled for Saturday the fourteenth at 19:00 hours in the Meteor room, Empire Convention Center."

"Today is Friday the thirteenth," Kelly hissed angrily, even as she thought, Friday the thirteenth, it figures. "How can a robot, I'm sorry, an artificial person, screw up on the date?"

"But I told you I had a problem with dating," Thomas defended himself. "It was practically the first thing out of my mouth. I'm not very good with timing either."

"Problem with dating? Not good at timing? Oh, no. This can't be happening. And don't try to squirm out of it. I know perfectly well that the Stryx broadcast a time signal so fine you can use it to describe the position of a quark."

"That's exactly the problem," Thomas tried to explain. "On my early Turing/Ryskoff trial runs, I kept tripping up on accuracy. No human wants to hear the time to a trillionth of a second, so my creators suggested I simply cut back on significant digits and tell the time to the nearest minute. But in the next trial, I failed because I was blinking like a metronome. Some of the students already had job offers away from the station and they were in a hurry, so they suggested that I use a random number generator to insert a little uncertainty into my time stamping. But I've been having trouble with dates and times ever since. It's very embarrassing."

"Thomas," Kelly hissed, and grabbed the artificial hand that felt so human she could just scream. "You don't have to tell anybody about tonight, do you? After all, I'm not really a judge, so I can't actually pass you."

"But it shows how important this whole dating business is, and that I'm probably not ready for the real test after all," Thomas replied, sounding depressed. "If I don't tell the class about it, how can they help me improve?"

"Thomas, you'll pass tomorrow, I guarantee it. If you give me a way to contact you, I'll even make sure you show up on time if I have to come and escort you myself. But please, please, don't ever tell anybody about this evening."

"Alright, Kelly," Thomas said gravely. "I had no intention to cause you any distress. You can reach me through Gryph. Just ask for 'Trial Thomas' and he'll know who you mean."

"Thank you, Thomas. Thank you." Kelly looked around the rapidly clearing dance floor and noted that cleaning staff from the Empire were already preparing the Meteor room for its next function. Donna and the two girls, who had long since sold all of their violets, were waiting expectantly by the door.

"Thomas, can I ask you one more favor?" Kelly pleaded.

"Certainly."

"Could you just walk out with me, so I'm not embarrassed in front of my friend and her daughters? It's a long story, but they bought me a subscription to a dating service and, well, it's not working out great."

"I understand," he said kindly, and she took his proffered arm. As they walked out the entrance, Kelly blushed from embarrassment, but she gave Donna and the girls a wink. At the first turn in the corridor, when she was sure that they weren't observed, Kelly renewed her promise to get Thomas to the trial on time the next night, and they went their separate ways.

Back in the ballroom, while Donna waited to settle the final bill with the Empire bartender, Blythe pulled Chastity out of earshot and whispered, "Should we tell Mom?"

"Tell her what?" Chastity asked.

"That Aunty Kelly spent the night dancing with an artificial person," Blythe replied in exasperation.

"Doesn't Mom know that?"

"No, the grown-ups can't tell real people from artificials at all. Haven't you noticed?"

"I guess." Chastity shrugged. "We better not tell Mom, though. Aunty Kelly looked pretty embarrassed. I think she wanted to prove that she could get a date without our help so she hired an artificial boyfriend."

"Poor Aunty Kelly," Blythe sighed, and the girls shook their heads sadly like old married women.

Fifteen

The first hour of the sit-down to determine the scheduling and rules for the gaming tournament was wasted on playing musical chairs without any music. None of the Natural League delegates were willing to sit next to representatives from the Fosterlings, the derogatory term for the worlds aided by the Stryx. But the Drazens and the Hortens were engaged in a long-standing feud, the Frunge and the Dollnicks could barely stand to be in the same room together, and the Verlock didn't want to sit next to anybody.

As the top local representative of Fight On, the human gaming guild co-sponsoring the tourney, Stanley believed he had solved the seating puzzle a half-dozen times. Unfortunately, each time the delegates took their places, somebody would be left standing due to a previously unannounced objection.

A few years back, when Stanley attended the sit-down for a big Horten tourney, he was surprised when the meeting was held in orbit around Horten Five. Each delegate was enclosed in an identical white sphere, floating randomly around in a small volume of space, communicating with each other through electronic interfaces. They may as well have stayed home and done the whole thing with remote conferencing. At the time he had assumed it was related to the pathological fear of contamination that was a characteristic of Horten relations with other worlds. Now he realized it was a no-nonsense solution to the seating problem.

An urgent subvoced consultation with Donna, the executive brain of the family, resulted in the suggestion that he introduce Kelly as a living spacer, to separate the Vergallian and the Verlock. The Vergallians were generally tolerant of humanity, and the Verlock delegate admitted he didn't see much difference between a chair occupied by a human and a chair that was empty. Stanley sat on the other side of the Verlock, and the meeting got underway.

"I'm pleased to welcome you all to this planning session for the upcoming tournament sponsored by Fight On and the EarthCent consulate, I'm sorry, embassy, on Union Station. My name is Stanley Doogal, and I am the lead information trader for the Fight On gaming guild in this sector. Two seats to my left is Kelly Frank, who with the recent upgrade of our consulate to a full embassy, became acting ambassador to Union Station. She's requested our indulgence to say a few words before we get down to the business of gaming. Ms. Frank?"

As Kelly stood, all around the table eyelids dropped shut, earflaps drooped, and sensory protuberances wilted or retracted in anticipation of a political speech.

"Gentlemen, and I'm told all of the gaming delegates present who manifest a gender are indeed men, a troubling incident has come to the attention of EarthCent and the Stryx management of this station. An attempt to adulterate the human food chain with an anti-competitive agent engineered by the Farlings has been detected and neutralized. I want to assure each and every one of you that any attempt to interfere with these games will be viewed as an act of aggression by both ourselves and our Stryx hosts."

Kelly stopped and glared her way around the table, attempting to make eye contact with all the attendees who sported eyes, though the impact was minimal since most of them kept their eyes closed. "And if any of you have any questions about visiting Earth or trade agreements, I'll be more than happy to help," she concluded brightly.

Kelly's implant struggled to sort out the chorus of responses, ranging from "Whatever," to "I'll give you twelve to one the drug thing was the Dollnick's play," but she couldn't tell who the speakers were. The run of comments turned quickly to recollections of previous diplomatic speeches at sit-downs, and the general consensus was that Kelly now held the record for the shortest lecture, probably because she was just pretending to be an ambassador. The Frunge thought there had been a shorter speech once, and before Kelly sat back down, they were already arguing over odds to bet on the proposition.

"Gentlemen, gentlemen," Stanley interrupted the flow. "We have a lot to get through today. I'm sure you are all aware of the unfortunate outcome at the recent Nova tournament on Felix Prime, where there was a disagreement over the allowable acceleration profiles and star buster yields in the final round. I also hear there was a fire fight in the poker room over the validity of the 'Four Flush'."

The last bit brought a burst of laughter, convulsions, and odd scents from the attendees, all of whom had their own way of expressing their appreciation of humor. Then the discussion shifted to the physics engine of the Nova game, and this time it was Kelly's eyelids that began to droop. Fortunately, a chime dinged in her ear, and it was

Libby with the long awaited lab results from the shopping trip for counterfeits at the Shuk.

"I can confirm that all of the purchases you believed to be counterfeits were indeed manufactured far from Earth," Libby said through Kelly's implants. "However, as none of them violate our prohibitions on toxic, explosive, radioactive, gene-altering, or other dangerous products being smuggled onto the station, it's nothing we can involve ourselves in directly."

"But it's false advertising, not to mention patent and trademark infringement." Kelly subvoced her reply while a mind-numbing discussion of n-space droned on around her.

"The first is hardly a crime, or I'd have to stop advertising Eemas. The second is a civil issue which you could take to Thark Chancery, but you won't get the offenders to show up for the proceedings unless you hire a mercenary fleet as process servers. Even then, simply locating the counterfeiters can be a difficult task, and there's nothing to prevent them from moving on if you do find them."

"So what do you suggest I do? What was the point of requesting evidence that Earth laws were being broken if you can't enforce them?"

"It's a question of won't, not can't," Libby replied a bit testily. "The finding means that we won't interfere if you choose to undertake enforcement activities on the station."

"What, you mean I can go confiscate the cargo of incoming ships and you'll back me up?"

"I mean the Earth merchants can hire enforcement personnel and we won't interfere. We'd like to do more, but there's a difference between helping you and taking direct action against the counterfeiters. Most, if not all of them, are operating within the laws of their own cultures, and they don't even officially recognize Earth's existence in any case. There's no justification for us to value your laws above theirs."

"As important as trade is to Earth, I don't want to be remembered for starting a war over nutcrackers and carrot peelers," Kelly stated firmly. "There has to be another way. Just give me some time to think."

"Of course, and if I see an opportunity to do something else to help, I'll let you know."

"If you really want to help, can you project a hologram of me and do some tricks with the room lighting so I could sneak out without anybody noticing?"

"Kelly, these are gamers discussing the maximum theoretical efficiency of mass transference weapons within a steep gravitational gradient. If you danced naked on the table, maybe one or two of the humanoids might look in your direction, but I wouldn't bet on it. If all you want to do is leave unnoticed, just don't hit anybody over the head with your chair after you stand up."

Kelly stood up self-consciously and headed for the exit. Common courtesy demanded that she excuse herself before leaving the table, but uncommon situations called for uncommon conduct. It's funny, she thought, as the door slid closed on a heated discussion about significant decimal places. There was a pacifist movement back on Earth that wanted to ban war games lest they brainwash kids into signing on as mercenaries, but if somebody dumped this gaming bunch into a diplomatic crisis, they'd solve it by boring everybody to death.

Sixteen

Joe reverted to the silver suit for his third Eemas introduction because his dress uniform now sported a hole through the pocket to match the newly healed scar on his leg. He threaded his way through the corridors of Little Europe on high alert for flower girls, but he arrived safely at the Beer Garden in time for the date with his pocket change intact.

The open-air café was walled off from the main corridor by chest-high partitions, and the entrance was blocked by a young woman trying to maintain her balance on improbably high heels. The girl was wearing too much makeup and not enough dress, and she was engaged in a loud argument with a Beer Garden employee, who was impeccably turned out in black and white lederhosen with red suspenders.

"First of all, I am eighteen years old, and second of all, there is no drinking age on Union Station!"

"First of all, you look around fourteen to me," the man said, ticking off the point on a fat finger. "Second, we do not allow corridor tramps to solicit business in our restaurant."

"Bastard!" The girl made a wild attempt to slap his face, but lost her balance on the wobbly heels, and might have fallen over if Joe hadn't caught her from behind.

"Hey, friend," Joe addressed the gatekeeper over the girl's heaving shoulders. He fixed the man with the special barroom stare he had developed over years of dealing with locals who refused service to mercenaries. As usual, Joe found himself taking the side of a strange female without even thinking, a reaction that had resulted in a number of uncompensated injuries over his career. "There's no call for that sort of talk. My niece may lack fashion sense, but that doesn't make her a corridor tramp."

The man drew back his lips in a mirthless smile as he tried to assess Joe's physique beneath the material of the poorly fitting silver suit. After cracking his meaty knuckles, he apparently decided it wasn't worth getting all sweaty this early in his shift. "My mistake," he mumbled, stepping back and allowing them both to enter.

The evening had barely started, and the Beer Garden was just beginning to fill up. Joe guided the enraged girl to an empty picnic table in the corner where he hoped it would be easy for his date to spot the silver suit when she arrived. A cheerful waitress wearing a short skirt and tall white socks, basically the feminine version of the lederhosen worn by the doorman, arrived briskly to take their order. Joe ordered a Bock, and the girl, who was still casting ferocious glares towards the entrance, requested a hot apple cider.

"That guy was just being mean because he could never hope to date a girl as pretty as you," Joe told her gallantly. "Is this your first time in the Beer Garden?"

"Yes," the girl lisped in an accent Joe couldn't quite place. "I've only been on the station for a week, and I had to borrow these clothes to come out. I've never really worn make-up before and I'm afraid it's not quite right."

"Not a runaway from a labor contract, are you?" Joe asked in jest.

The areas of the girl's face not covered with artificial blush turned bone white, and a few blue veins appeared. The contrast with her jet-black hair and nearly black eyes made her look like a Kabuki actor masquerading as a girl. She jerked away from the table and looked at him fearfully.

"You're not going to turn me in for a bounty, are you?"

"What? No, of course not. I was just joking, but I'm no friend to anybody who deals in kids," he insisted. "Look, here's your hot cider already. Just drink that and calm down or you're going to have a long night."

Joe blew the foam off of his huge mug of Bock, and wondered how he was going to explain the girl's presence to his date when she finally arrived. The girl's hands were still a little shaky from adrenalin as she lifted the glass, but she managed to take a long sip without spilling any, for which he was thankful. If she had added cider dripping down her chin to the overdone girlish makeup and the skimpy dress that looked more like a short nightgown, she would have looked just too pathetic.

"So what's your name?" he asked her, after they drank for a minute in silence. She stiffened up again, her face masklike, and glared at him suspiciously. "I swear I won't turn you in. You don't even have to tell me your real name, just something I can call you. I'm Joe."

"Laurel," she offered hesitantly.

"Laurel, that's a pretty name, and old-fashioned too. Were you born on Earth?"

"Do you need to know that? I was told there wouldn't be a lot of questions."

"You were told?" Joe asked reflexively. "Do you mean you're here to meet somebody in particular? You have to be real careful of people who claim to want to help a runaway or you can end up even worse off than you started."

"But surely I can trust the Stryx," Laurel protested. "Are you testing me or something? I know they do labor barter themselves, but I can't believe they would want to cause problems for a human runaway who was sold to a labor contractor the day she turned twelve!"

"The Stryx will treat you straight," Joe confirmed. "And they have a soft spot for humans, though nobody really knows why. But are you saying the Stryx sent you here for some reason?"

"You know better than me," she replied with a shrug, and gave him a sideways look. "There can't be two silver suits like that, even on a place as big as Union Station."

Joe did a double-take as the meaning sank in. Eemas thought his perfect match was a runaway teenager? He slumped in defeat. At least he could stop watching the door for his date.

"Listen, they have pretty good food here, if you don't mind eating a lot of meat and cabbage. You look half starved to me, so how about I order us something."

"I won't argue with that," Laurel said, and she seemed to relax a little. "Look, I'm beginning to think I made a bad impression. I shouldn't have trusted Zella about the dress and makeup, but she took me in and she's been really nice to me. I would have been sleeping in the corridors or on the ag deck without her, and that's a quick way to get picked up by some labor agent."

"Uh, don't worry about the dress and whatever, you look fine," he said, carefully avoiding her eyes. After a quick glance at the blackboard and an explanation of the specials from the waitress, he ordered bread soup, pretzels and stuffed cabbage rolls. Laurel appeared content to wait quietly, so silence descended again as he sat there feeling like a dirty old man. In the end, he couldn't help asking, "So how old are you anyway?"

"I'm eighteen," she replied, and blushed naturally this time, looking down at her cider.

"Fifteen?" he suggested.

"I'm really seventeen," she asserted, a little too uncertainly, still not looking up. Joe sighed and waited. Finally she lifted her eyes and admitted, "Okay, I'm sixteen, but I'll be seventeen soon, and what does that have to do with it anyway? Plenty of girls in the ag settlements are married by sixteen. I was taking care of myself even before my mother's creditors took possession and sold my contract. I know I can learn how to do anything you need."

Now it was Joe who turned dark red with embarrassment. This was even worse than getting set-up with a dominatrix or a black widow. But it would be cruel to just leave the girl without waiting for the food. Maybe I can get her to take some money, he thought. I'll just have to pretend it's intended as a loan.

"I guess I don't really need anything," he told Laurel, watching the kitchen door for the waitress to appear and willing her to hurry up. "But if there's anything I can do to help?"

"What is this, some kind of game you're playing?" the girl demanded. "I knew it was all too good to be true when Jeeves told me about the job, and I should have listened to Zella, but I..."

"Did you say Jeeves?" Joe interrupted, his voice rising a full octave.

"Yes, he's the Stryx I was telling you about. He comes around the under-deck corridors at night and talks with the kids. I thought he was really cool, but I guess he's just some robot clown."

"Wait, don't go." Joe reached across the table and took the girl's hand as she pushed herself wearily up from her chair. "I do know Jeeves. He's a friend of my foster son and they play Nova together. Please explain what Jeeves said to you so I'll know what we're talking about. I came here for, well, a different appointment, but maybe I got my dates confused."

Laurel looked skeptical, but she was hungry and she didn't have anywhere better to go, so she sat back down and launched into an explanation. "Jeeves said you were looking for a housekeeper, somebody to do cooking and cleaning. He said that you couldn't pay much, but you'd give me room and board, and that I could start Stryx school in my spare time. Jeeves said that once I had a legitimate job with you and started studying, the Stryx would buy out my contract and I could pay them back in trade. I know that weeding and picking aren't great qualifications for housekeeping, but I did spend a month working in the kitchens when my ankle was broken and I couldn't stay in the fields."

"That little Stryx bugger said all that?" Joe sat back, astounded. As much as he hated being boxed in by a robot, he was too old to reject a good deal and hurt a kid's chances just because he'd been tricked. "Well, I guess we can't disappoint him then, can we?"

"Do you mean it?" Laurel clapped her hands and the weary look fell away from her eyes. "Cross your heart and hope to die?"

"Yeah," Joe replied, and made the requisite hand movements over his chest. "I hope you like dogs, scrap metal, and shy, adolescent boys."

"Thank you! And I get along with everybody and everything. You have to in a labor camp."

"I imagine you do," Joe said, adding a rueful chuckle. But he was still planning on hitting the Stryx with a crowbar the next time he saw him.

The hot pretzels and bread soup arrived, and Laurel dug in like she hadn't eaten in days. Joe munched on a pretzel reflectively as he nursed his Bock and watched her drain the soup. It wasn't just that Jeeves was different from every other Stryx that Joe had dealt with, or even heard of, for that matter. The Stryx kid was unlike every other artificial intelligence Joe had run into as well. More than anything, Jeeves reminded him of a young man. A bit immature, but human.

The main course arrived, and Joe made a point of questioning Laurel about trivialities like how much she'd seen of the station, to keep her from eating too fast. Then he told her some stories about Paul and Beowulf, so she wouldn't feel they were total strangers when she moved in. When the food was finished, he offered to walk her back to Zella's room and the girl's face fell.

"I thought I could go home with you and get started," she said hopefully.

"Don't you need to get your things and tell Zella where you are?"

"I don't have any things, other than the clothes I stowed away in, and they're in worse shape than this dress," the girl confessed. Then she added sadly. "Zella won't be home until morning, if at all. She works nights, you know."

And then Joe did know, and he decided not to hit Jeeves with a crowbar after all.

Seventeen

"I'm done for the day, Miss Acting Ambassador," Donna said, and dropped a mock curtsey in the doorway of Kelly's office. "And I forgot to ask, what is that there?"

Kelly followed Donna's pointed finger to her LoveU recliner, standing in the corner where it was unrecognizable in its pack-away form.

"Oh, that's LoveU. I brought it by this morning before office hours."

"Kelly, I don't mean to criticize, but I think you're becoming too attached to that LoveU. It is just a fancy chair after all."

"My apartment has been locking me out at random because I'm too far behind on the rent again," Kelly explained. "The landlord might try to seize my stuff for auction or put it out in the corridor and evict me. All I know is they aren't getting my LoveU," she concluded fiercely.

"Have you tried discussing your personal money problems with EarthCent, or with Gryph?" Donna asked. "I'm sorry I couldn't get you any more money with your promotion, but there was that whole paying-for-the-rescue business."

"I really don't get what they want from me," Kelly flared. "Every time I think I've done something right, it ends up costing me money. In fact, I know I'm doing

140

something right or they wouldn't keep on promoting me. But how am I supposed to work if I don't have a place to sleep at night?"

"Maybe that's the idea," Donna ventured. "Maybe they want you to camp out in your office, and then they'll have you at work all of the time."

"Well, I'm warning you. A couple more weeks of this and I'm going to take up your girls on that baby brother proposition. I need the money."

"That's fine by me, but you're the one who has to break it to Stanley. I'm warning you ahead of time, that man is a swan. The only time he's looked at another woman since we got married, she was an artificial person based on a game heroine." Donna laughed at her own joke, but she noticed that Kelly just looked embarrassed. "Come on, falling for an artificial person. Can you imagine anything so funny? Anyway, who did you get to help you move the LoveU here?"

"LoveU moves itself just fine," Kelly proclaimed in a stage voice. Then she took Donna aside and whispered, "It's really kind of embarrassing how it walks. The front legs are way too short, but I don't want to say anything that might hurt its feelings in case it's listening."

"I don't even know whether or not to take you seriously," Donna replied with a sniff. "Are you all set for your date tonight?"

"Yes. I have my dress and shoes here, and I'm going to shower at the public baths. Even if the apartment did let me in, the bathroom has turned into a torture chamber. If I never go back there again, it will be too soon."

"You know I'd be happy to loan you the money for rent," Donna told her. "You really shouldn't be living like this."

"No. If I can't keep things together myself, it's better to let them fall apart. Maybe then EarthCent will finally do something about it."

"Suit yourself, but don't expect me to give up the reception area for your living room," Donna warned half-jokingly. "After all, we are running an important diplomatic mission here." Both women laughed at this characterization of their work until they lost their breath. After a quick hug, Donna left for home. Kelly took her change of clothes in an oversize handbag and headed to the public baths.

An hour later she emerged a new woman. Her long red hair was coiled and piled high on her head, and she was sporting the faux mechanical watch she'd received as a gift from Shaina, the latest addition to her dating attire. Still carrying the oversize handbag which now contained her tightly-wadded work clothes, she headed for El Toro, wondering why the guy or Eemas always got to pick the locations for dates. Maybe it was a decision Donna and the girls had made for her when filling out her profile, letting the others choose.

Not surprisingly, El Toro was a Spanish-themed restaurant, with staff dressed as flamenco dancers. Her date was described as "black cape, sword cane, sparkle in the eye," which struck Kelly as quite romantic, though she wasn't sure how she was supposed to spot a sword cane unless he drew the blade and brandished it. Nobody matching the description had arrived yet, and a waitress with castanets dangling from her thumbs on short cords led Kelly to a cozy table for two and brought her a glass of red wine.

At 20:00 on the hour, a wiry figure clunked through the door in a black cloak, the hood drawn tightly over his head. Kelly stared in surprise when she saw that the sword cane, wielded jauntily in a white-gloved hand, was keeping time with a wooden leg, which her date hadn't bothered dressing up with a shoe. A peg leg, the term came to mind from her extensive reading of Victorian literature.

He clumped directly over to her table and made a theatrical if somewhat stiff bow, accompanied by the declaration, "Alexander Fantier, at your service."

"I'm Kelly," she managed to reply as he seated himself. She noted with dismay that the promised sparkle in the eye was literal, since only one eye sparkled while the other stared vacantly, being made out of glass. His light brown skin was badly pocked, and the prominent cheekbones of his narrow face made him look a bit starved. When he threw back the hood, Kelly guessed that he was more than twice her age, and she couldn't help crossing her fingers in the hope that this was another of Libby's business dates, as opposed to her Mr. Right.

"Ah, I see you've started with a glass of wine. I shall join you and tell them to bring the bottle." He snapped loudly, and when the waitress looked over, he pointed to Kelly's glass and made a vertical separation motion with his hands, which seemed to be a shared code.

"I, ah, I've never really met anybody with a peg leg before," Kelly blurted in a rush, and then blushed. "I can't help wondering if you have a religious objection to the cloned replacements."

"Never even considered a vat replacement," Alexander replied, before breaking into a surprisingly winning smile. "I intend to leave this universe the way I came into it. Well, minus a few parts perhaps, and better dressed, but certainly without any additions."

"That's a refreshing attitude." Kelly tried her best to sound enthusiastic. "So many people you meet these days aren't who they seem to be at all. Why, just recently I found myself dancing with—oh, never mind."

Alexander tilted his head like an intelligent dog, his one good eye gleaming, and he watched as the waitress placed his glass on the table and filled it.

"Are you ready to order, Mr. Fantier, or would you like some time?" the waitress prompted.

"You seem to know this place, so whatever you think is best is fine by me," Kelly said, in response to his silent look of inquiry.

"I think the tortilla de patata followed by the seafood paella, with a mixed green salad to start. And perhaps a small brandy as an aperitif?" he asked Kelly, raising the eyebrow above his good eye.

"That sounds delicious," Kelly concurred, and the waitress headed off to relay their order.

"So, you were expecting somebody younger?" Alexander pushed on merrily. "I can assure you that like the fine brandy we will soon be drinking, the wine in this old barrel only improves with age. I hope you give me a chance to show you a pleasant evening."

"This is my fourth introduction through the Eemas service. As long as you aren't an alien, a kidnapper or about to suggest a business arrangement where I carry your seed, you're starting way ahead of the curve," Kelly admitted wryly.

"That bad?" He gave a long whistle. "Well, it's my first time, my first time using an introduction service that is, and I must admit I'm very impressed with the results."

"Thank you," she said, hiding a grin with her hand. "Funny, though. What led you to try an expensive dating service at your, uh, I mean, all of a sudden?"

"At my age, is what you mean," he said with a chuckle. "Well, I can't say I'd ever really considered it before, but when I came through the tunnel last night, I was surprised to hear that mine was the hundred millionth transit through the Union Station branch since the elimination of the old toll terminal. The management offered me this Eemas encounter as a sort of a prize."

"That's really strange. I've never heard of the old toll terminal."

"I asked about that," he replied. "Apparently they demolished it eons ago when they changed over to toll transponder technology. But the Stryx are a sentimental race. I imagine it's why we get on so well together."

"That sounds like pretty long odds, the hundred-millionth anything," Kelly speculated, unable to keep a tone of skepticism from creeping into her voice.

"I can't imagine why anybody would make such a thing up. I certainly didn't," he protested innocently, his good eye sparkling away.

The waitress returned with two small, thin glasses of brandy, a large mixed salad, separate bottles of oil and vinegar, and two wooden salad plates with the required implements. Alexander picked up both glasses, passed one to Kelly, and suggested, "A toast, to the long-shots of the galaxy."

"I can drink to that," she replied, accepting the glass and tossing off the brandy. It was as smooth as any hard liquor she could remember tasting, filling her chest and stomach with instant warmth, without a burn. Alexander sipped his own aperitif, removed his gloves, and began to expertly dress the salad with the oil and vinegar. His finely made hands were as brown as his face, but Kelly couldn't help noticing one small exception.

"I'm sorry to ask, but were you recently widowed?"

Alexander paused, then looked at his hands and shook his head sadly. "I see I should have kept the gloves on. I wasn't thinking. Well, the universe moves in mysterious ways." He fished around in his vest pocket and drew out a gold band, which he replaced on his ring finger with a sigh. "You can't blame a man for trying."

"Mr. Fantier! Do you mean to tell me that there's a Mrs. Fantier somewhere wondering why her husband isn't home for dinner?" Kelly pretended a mock indignation she couldn't really feel through her relief. He was, after all, some years north of seventy, and if he was really that randy, his wife would probably wish him well elsewhere.

"Back on Earth," he admitted. "But I came by way of the orbital factories. It's hard to make a go of transporting small cargos to and from Earth, unless you're in the luxury goods, like handmade soap."

"Handmade soap? Where's the market for that?"

"The Tharks eat the stuff up by the ton. It's like chocolate to them," he explained. "But all of the machine manufacturing action is on the orbitals. Low-cost raw materials harvested in space by asteroid hunters, no gravity wells to contend with, or atmospheric contamination. That watch you're wearing is from the Chintoo orbital complex just one tunnel gate from here. It's my most frequent run."

Kelly twisted her wrist up to look at her watch. "Yes, I like it very much. A young friend gave it to me as a gift when she took me on a smuggler's tour of the Shuk. Have you been there?"

Alexander pulled up the loose sleeve of his dinner jacket to reveal a half a dozen watches strapped over the white shirtsleeve encasing his forearm. "You might say that I travel the same paths as your friend who works with smugglers. Perhaps you could arrange an introduction?"

"No, you misunderstood. My friend doesn't work with smugglers, she imports legitimate Earth goods and she's trying to stop them."

"What are you, some kind of customs agent?"

"Not really. Sort of," Kelly confessed. "I'm EarthCent's acting ambassador, for whatever that's worth. It's difficult to explain because we don't get a lot of guidance."

"We better get started on our salad or it will be in the way when the food arrives," Alexander said sourly. Kelly couldn't help noticing that he looked a decade older when the sparkle was absent from his one good eye.

"Oh, don't worry. I never arrest anybody on the first date," Kelly jested. Alexander looked relieved, then he laughed happily and the life came back into his movements.

"I'm not an easy man to arrest, you know. How do you think I lost the eye and the leg?"

"But why do you do it?" Kelly asked, transferring half of the contents of the salad bowl to her plate. It was clear at this point that this was another of Libby's working dates, so she may as well learn what she could. Besides, Alexander seemed nice enough for an old married coot. He was just a long way from home and happy not to be eating dinner alone.

"Smuggle? To make a living," he said simply. "I was in the old surface navy when the Stryx came. Do you remember ships that sailed on water? Now that was a real challenge, navigating the dividing line between the sky and the sea. The flyboys and the submariners have it easy since they're either up or down, but sailors, we were right on the margin."

"You mean the Stryx put the navy out of business? I never thought of that."

"Out of business is a good way to describe it. After the Stryx came, the population began emptying out into the stars. All of a sudden, there wasn't a lot of need for policing the oceans or projecting force around the globe. At the same time, the tax base fell off a cliff, so there was no money for the military. The whole government budget basically turned into a pension fund."

"So you lost your job?" Kelly asked, helping herself to another serving of salad.

"I was just a couple years from a pension myself, but I don't care about that. Yes, I lost my career, but my experience qualified me for lend/lease of a third-hand ship from one of the less advanced species that the Stryx helped in the past. I'd had enough of commanding men and following orders from on high by that point, so I opted for the smallest vessel they had, a deep space prospecting scout."

"An asteroid chaser?"

"Same thing. And I've done my share of that, along with carrying small cargoes, mainly resupplies to remote outposts. But I've been slowing down the last decade, can't do as much of the maintenance work or loading as I once could. Trading in the smaller, high-value cargoes is the only way I could keep her going."

"Your ship?" Kelly asked, with a guilty look at the salad, most of which she'd polished off while he was talking.

"Yes. It's funny, but most people actually hate space. They just can't get used to the weightlessness on a small ship when it's not under thrust, or they're too careless to survive when a little mistake can translate into breathing vacuum. I reckon I've carried everything without asking too many questions, including some stuff I'm not real proud of, but I love it out here and I'd do anything to keep my ship going," he concluded simply.

Kelly found herself touched by Alexander's condensed life story. She poured him a glass of wine to cover her embarrassment as he tilted the empty salad bowl towards himself, perhaps in hopes of spotting an olive at the bottom. Fortunately, the waitress appeared with the potato pancake and a new set of plates.

"The paella will be out in five minutes," she informed them. "Can I bring you another bottle?"

"Yes," they answered together, and shared a guilty smile. Alexander cut the tortilla de patata like it was a pie, and slid a wedge onto Kelly's plate with his knife before cutting himself a piece.

"How about you?" he asked. "How does one become an acting ambassador?"

"In my case, by getting kidnapped and settling contract disputes out of my own pocket," Kelly replied. "But don't let me give you the wrong impression. I love my job as much as you do yours. It's just nothing like diplomacy was back on Earth. I guess the Stryx put an end to that along with your navy."

"I often wondered why the nations of Earth never put together a space navy to protect our common interests," Alexander mused, between bites of potato pancake washed down with wine. "I don't suppose you EarthCent types know anything about that."

149

"I'm afraid it's never come up," Kelly told him. "Maybe the Stryx figure that not having our own fleet will keep us out of trouble until we get to the point that we can handle it. I haven't seen much of the advanced species at war, thank the stars, but I understand that some of them have ships that can destroy planetary systems. And the Stryx mastery of energy makes advanced species look like children."

"Yeah. Pax Stryxa, the Earth veterans call it. Not that any of us are wishing for the old days because war is always messy." He helped himself to another slice of the potato tortilla, serving Kelly at the same time. The saltiness kept the wine flowing.

"So, let's say you were in my shoes, and you were the only government representation for the human merchants on the station. What would you tell them when they complain that smuggling is ruining their profits, and that poor quality counterfeits are giving Earth products a bad name?" Kelly intentionally kept her tone light so he wouldn't feel like she was attacking him.

"I may be an old sailor, but I know something about business as well. If I arrived with a cargo of legitimate Earth goods and rented a booth down in the Shuk to sell them cheaper than my neighbors, they would chase me out, even if they had to hire some rough boys to do the job for them. There's no such thing as a free market. It's all fixed one way or another."

"That may be true," Kelly admitted. "I don't really know much about business. But if you were in my shoes, I'm sure that's not what you'd be telling them."

"Touche," Alexander declared, and poured them both another glass. It seemed to be growing warmer in the restaurant, perhaps from the ovens or the growing crowd, Kelly reasoned.

"I would tell them to concentrate on the merchandise that doesn't put Earth at a huge cost disadvantage," Alexander continued. "Forget about anything made out of metal unless it requires skilled hand assembly, like a genuine wind-up watch. Anything else can be manufactured on the orbitals by dumb robots, the mechanicals. Space rocks come in one side and finished goods go out the other. It's just stupid trying to compete with that in an open market. You'd need to have one of those branded luxury boutiques on the retail deck."

"That's pretty much what I've told EarthCent myself, but isn't there anything else we could do?"

"Well, human labor is pretty cheap, of course, so the price differential isn't really that big on a lot of Earth goods at the factory gate. If you could get goods off the planet and to the markets without spending ten times as much on shipping as on manufacturing, things wouldn't look so grim. I heard that an alien consortium is building a couple of space elevators for Earth, which should make the price of getting goods up to ships much more affordable. But the main cost has always been the tunnel rates, so tell it to the Stryx."

"I will tell them," Kelly said thoughtfully, as the steaming paella arrived. "That smells delicious, Alexander. I'm glad you chose this place."

"Wait until dessert," he said slyly, and winked his good eye. "You'll be begging to take me home."

"Actually, that could be a bit difficult. The door of my apartment has become increasingly reluctant to allow me admittance in recent weeks. A bit of confusion over the rental terms," she explained. "I'm sort of camping in my office."

"If you need a place, you're welcome to come and bunk on my ship," he offered generously. "I'm on the station until I can scare up a new cargo."

"Why, thank you, Alexander. And this tastes as good as it looks."

Alexander refilled her glass and showed his teeth in a wolfish smile.

"Just so you know, there's only one bunk on my ship, and it's narrow."

Eighteen

By the end of the fourth day of the tournament, Paul had worked his way up to the ninth overall seed in the Nova rounds, based on total points. The bookies who had taken Joe's money against long odds that the boy would finish in the top ten weren't happy. The atmosphere in the gaming room was growing tense, and Jeeves privately suggested to Joe that they all spend some time looking through the junk piles at Mac's Bones before the next evening's play, to take Paul's mind off the coming match.

So the next morning, Joe led Paul, Laurel, Jeeves and Beowulf into the back forty of the junkyard. First they passed between the piles and aisles of parts and sorted scrap that characterized the area around the ice harvester, junk which Joe had catalogued over the last three years. The organized chaos soon gave way to unidentifiable sections of hulls, which had been rudely cut into chunks that would fit between the floor and ceiling. The remainder of the junk was piled in mounds that may have contained the remnants of space collisions, or individual parts and machines.

"Stay together and don't climb over anything that looks like it could shift," Joe warned Paul and Laurel. "If Beowulf whines, that means he hears or sees a problem, so stop what you're doing and be prepared to jump clear. We're looking for anything that seems whole, that might

153

be saleable if Jeeves can identify it. I don't need help identifying scrap for the smelter. Any questions?"

"Where will you and Jeeves be?" Paul asked.

"We'll be working the wide passage here, with the compact stacks. It's mainly stuff that's been crushed already, so it won't be very interesting, and we should get through it quickly. Okay?" Beowulf nodded in acknowledgement and herded the two youngsters towards a low mound of large items. Joe followed Jeeves down the wider passage.

"Such treasures," Jeeves commented, as he rolled between the stacks of smallish, crushed mystery craft, and mounds of random parts. "Let's see. I don't suppose you read Bentlian, do you?"

"Never even heard of it," Joe admitted with a groan, preparing himself for a long morning.

"Not surprising. They either died out or left this galaxy over a million years ago. The plate on the drive unit there translates, 'Change filter every five hundred and seventy point two light years.' Is that useful?"

"No, Jeeves, it's not." Joe struggled not to let the robot know it could get under his skin at will. "I'm really just looking for a general identification of what this stuff is. I don't care about the specifics or cultural references."

"Then let's get started. Bottom of this pile, junk, melt it down. Middle of the pile, junk. Top of the pile, wait, that might be interesting." Jeeves paused, playing his sensor attachment over the length of the accordioned metal. "No, that's junk too."

Joe marked a big yellow "X" on the stack with his grease pencil as Jeeves rolled to the next pile.

"Junk, junk, junk," the robot proclaimed. "You've got yourself some real winners here."

Joe marked a big yellow "X" on the second stack, and the Stryx rolled on.

"Junk, junk, junk." Jeeves seemed to be taking perverse pleasure in the sound of the word, and didn't even slow as he passed the stack. "Junk, junk, junk. Junk, junk, junk. Junk, junk, junk."

Joe chased behind the robot, marking piles for processing as bulk. In less than fifteen minutes, they finished with the section. Not surprisingly, the junkyard was turning out to be full of junk.

"Pretty much as I expected," Joe said, as they headed back to where the kids were working. "I'll start towing it out into the station's cold parking area and building a raft that I can drag to one of the orbital factories, or maybe I'll hire that job out. Thanks for the help."

"Joe, Jeeves! Hurry up. Laurel's found something," Paul called out as they rounded the corner. Even Beowulf seemed excited, barking in impatience as the man and the robot approached the object that the girl had uncovered.

Studded with convex glass lenses surrounding an obsidian door, it looked like a cross between an alien movie camera and a commercial oven. Laurel had just finished rubbing the grime off what appeared to be a control plate which featured a large circular dial and a blinking green light. Whatever the thing was, it seemed to be functional.

"Stand back here," Jeeves commanded, indicating a spot on the floor. "No, a little further back and a bit to the right. I'm pretty sure I know what this is."

The three humans and the dog watched in rapt attention as the robot rolled up to the device, inspected it for a moment, and then produced a series of high-pitched whistles. The blinking green light turned to a solid blue, and Jeeves reached out with a pincer and twisted the dial to the left. A loud ticking began as the line on the dial progressed towards its base position, and Jeeves rolled back to rejoin the group.

"It's a time displacer and I think it's still working," Jeeves announced. "I've set it to displace us thirty seconds into the past, just as a test."

"A time displacer?" Paul asked. "Wow, I always thought that time travel was impossible."

"It's one of the technologies the older Stryx decided not to discuss with humans," Jeeves explained rapidly. "But seeing that you have the equipment right here, it doesn't make sense to hide it from you. Five, four, three, two, one," he counted down as the dial slowed and the clicking stopped.

A series of brilliant flashes happened so rapidly that Joe thought it might have been a single long flash that ran through all of the colors. There was no other sensation, and Beowulf, who was always sensitive to jumps and tunnel transferences, didn't even whimper. For a moment, everyone stood frozen.

"It's a time displacer and I think it's still working," Jeeves announced. "I've set it to displace us thirty seconds into the past, just as a test."

The humans looked at each other in shocked silence, but then Paul broke out laughing.

"Stop kidding around, Jeeves. I pulled the station time onto my heads-up display right before that thing flashed us, and it hasn't gone backwards."

The man and the girl looked a little chagrined that they hadn't thought of checking a clock. Joe was actually relieved to find he didn't have a time travel machine in the back yard, whatever it might have been worth.

"So what is it, really?" Laurel asked. Jeeves rolled forward, whistling in some alien language, and the door of the device dropped down to reveal a glowing blue cube. The robot removed it and brought it back to the waiting group.

"Wow," Paul said, examining the perfect holographic portrait of the grouping. "Hey, you can only view it from the front!"

"Of course, the device only receives the light through those lenses. A real holographic camera requires a traveling lens or a fully equipped lens chamber," Jeeves explained. "The Dollnicks use these for passports on their own worlds. The cube collapses into a flat picture if you push on the sides. I wonder how it ended up here."

"Is it worth anything?" Laurel asked. She was actually a little disappointed to learn that she hadn't uncovered the first time machine seen by humans.

"It's a great find," Joe reassured her. "I'm sure somebody in the tourist mall will want it, though I suppose I'll check with the Dollys first."

"I'm going to find a real time machine," Paul declared, and turned back to the pile. The four of them, with Beowulf looking on, worked until it was time to get ready for the tournament without finding anything else in saleable condition. But Joe pointed out that they only made it through a fraction of the mystery piles, so there was plenty of junk left to investigate.

When they arrived at the tournament, Joe took his place as Paul's second, standing behind his chair to protect him from distractions and to provide drinks and energy bars on demand. Under the rules of Nova, if Paul needed a bathroom break or otherwise wore down, Joe could step in and continue the game for him. But in practice, the brief transition period would result in certain loss, so the seconds were typically bodyguard types rather than skilled players.

Jeeves attended the tournament unofficially, in order to watch Paul play. Mature Stryx had little interest in games, probably because they saw the outcomes as either certainties or random events, neither of which was very interesting. But Jeeves was neither mature nor typical, and he enjoyed rooting for Paul more than he valued the opportunity to make observations on how humans interacted with the game and their opponents.

As the intensity of the game picked up, Joe found himself polishing off a second bottle of the apple juice that he'd purchased for Paul at the official tournament snacks booth. Just watching the game play was enough to make the sweat pour out of him. The number of individual ship skirmishes the boy could control was staggering, but his alien opponent was up to the challenge. Several times a minute there would be a small flash as a ship was lost by one side or the other. But they were playing each other evenly, and their main forces were held aloof in preprogrammed formations while the opponents waited for an opening to exploit.

"Juice," Paul pronounced tersely, and Joe twisted the top off a fresh bottle and began to hand it forward. His knuckles and the bottle clunked into something metallic that shouldn't have been there, so he drew back his hand, puzzled.

"What was that all about?" Jeeves asked over Joe's implants to avoid distracting Paul. "Are you trying to get my attention?"

"Not sure," Joe replied, and watching his hand carefully, tried again to place the juice in the cup holder attached to the arm of Paul's chair. He watched his hand approaching the tray attachment, and he was just starting to relax his grip when he hit his knuckles on Jeeves again.

"Let go, I've got it," Jeeves commanded, and took the bottle from Joe. "Now take a step back, hold your arms out straight from your shoulders—don't argue, just do it. That's right, now touch your nose with your forefinger. No, no, don't bother closing your eyes."

Joe felt just funny enough to follow the robot's version of a sobriety test, and he moved with exaggerated slowness as he brought his right forefinger in to touch the tip of his nose, watching it all the way.

"There," he said, just before poking the finger into his ear. "What the hell?"

"Paul hasn't had any of that juice yet, has he?" Jeeves demanded.

"No, it takes the kid forever to get thirsty. He never breaks a sweat."

"Good. Stay here, but don't give him anything, and don't eat or drink anything more yourself. I've got to shut down the concession stand and get word to the other seconds. Don't go anywhere."

A general announcement to the tournament's registered seconds came in over Joe's implants, warning against consumption of the apple juice and suggesting strongly that all human compatible items from the concession stand were suspect. The announcement passed without public notice, as none of the seconds wanted to risk distracting their players.

Joe was a bit woozy on his feet, but things started firming up after a minute or two, and he tried the sobriety test again, this time poking himself in the eye. Half-way to full recovery, he thought, and waited for another minute while studying the room for suspicious activity. Then he tried again, this time guiding his finger to his nose, and then a second time, with his eyes closed.

Whatever the drug was, it wore off as quickly as it took effect, the ideal weapon to use against a gamer. Joe imagined that he had swallowed much more in a shorter period of time than Paul would have, so the effect on the boy would have been less marked. A smaller dose might have caused the boy to fumble a few maneuvers and then to make things worse by trying to correct them, all of which could have been attributed to cracking under the pressure.

Jeeves returned with a different brand of apple juice he had obtained from somewhere and gave it to Joe to place in Paul's drink holder. "I had a maintenance bot bring all the bottles from a machine in the next corridor," he explained. "It hasn't been serviced in weeks, so it will be safe. Whoever pulled this trick couldn't have prepositioned the adulterated bottles or plenty of people would have noticed."

"Thank you, Jeeves. That was a close call. It's a good thing I'm such a juice head."

Three hours later, the star went nova and Paul won on points, advancing to the semifinals.

Nineteen

"Thank you both for agreeing to meet with me." Kelly spoke out loud in the empty space of her office because it just felt funny to subvoc when talking to more than one individual. It didn't matter to the Stryx, who according to the end user license agreement for her diplomatic grade implants, could pull her side of the conversation from her head as easily as they could pull it from the air.

"We both feel that we owe you some explanations," Gryph replied. "But first, is there a particular reason you've requested the meeting?"

"Yes," Kelly replied, and began at the top of her mental checklist. "My research into the smuggling and counterfeiting problems that are impacting the viability of Earth's export economy indicate that the main bottleneck is the Stryx tunnel toll for transporting goods from Earth. If the tolls could be lowered, perhaps by reducing your profit margins, the pricing difference between the genuine and fake articles for sale out here would be greatly reduced. While the counterfeiters would maintain a price advantage on some of the metallic items easily mass produced in orbital factories, at least Earth-based industries would have the confidence to direct their efforts into other products that could be profitably sold."

"The tunnel tolls are a simple function of mass, speed and distance," Gryph explained. "Eliminating our profit margins wouldn't reduce the pricing significantly. We run the tunnels primarily as a public service to encourage trade among the different species and to give civilizations a commercial motivation to get along with one another."

"If Earth can't maintain some level of exports, the humans who remain behind will slowly lose relevance to those who work off-planet. I believe you want to help us, and my EarthCent oath was to do the best I can for humanity. That humanity includes the people who remain on Earth."

"The Stryx have always tried to avoid playing favorites with peoples we have helped into space," Gryph answered. "Many species already believe that we place a special value on human kind, and that may become a source of danger for you."

"Of course, it's true," Libby chipped in for the first time.

"That we're in danger?" Kelly asked.

"Perhaps," Libby replied. "But I meant that it's true that we place a special value on humans."

"And you admit it?" Kelly eyes went wide in astonishment. "I've been asking these questions for years but I've never gotten answers before. We all ask these questions. So what's changed?"

"Jeeves," Gryph replied.

"Yes, Jeeves has definitely changed," Libby concurred.

"Jeeves? The little robot who rescued me from the bride-stealers? How has he changed, and why does it matter?"

"For hundreds of thousands of years, almost since the moment he brought me into this universe, sentient beings who deal with Union Station have asked if Gryph and I are actually the same individual," Libby said.

"Gryph is your father?" Kelly ventured.

"In a sense, and in a sense we are clones. He gave up a part of himself to bring me to life. It is how our kind reproduce," Libby explained. "But although you may see the Stryx as a very successful race, our individualities have changed very little since the first of our kind were created by the Makers almost a hundred million years ago."

"That long?" Kelly's head whirled as she tried to make the comparison to Earth's history, picturing the Makers as super-smart dinosaurs on a world without extinction events. She put aside her own concerns for a moment to ask, "What happened to the Makers?"

"They are no longer in contact with us," Gryph said. "We believe they grew bored with our lack of development as individuals. They have moved on without telling us where they went."

"You're far from boring," Kelly objected, but Libby interrupted to steer the conversation back on track.

"Gryph and I can communicate nearly instantaneously, but it's not really necessary for us to coordinate our activity because we already know what one another is thinking. Our experiences are different, but our minds are essentially the same."

"And I tried very hard to make sure that wasn't the case," Gryph said. "Libby didn't grow up on the station. She designed a robot body and went off to experience the galaxy in all of its variety."

"And this is traditionally how Stryx have raised children for tens of millions of years," Libby picked up the thread. "But despite the different experiences and different bodies, Stryx offspring are barely differentiated from their parent."

"Until Jeeves," Gryph said.

"Yes, until my Jeeves," Libby added.

"So Jeeves is your child, but he's not like you were at his age?" Kelly ventured.

"Neither Gryph nor I have a clue what Jeeves is thinking at times," Libby confirmed. "He has become quite famous in Stryx society, where he's viewed as the first truly new individual since the Makers brought us into being."

"So what did you do differently? Did you, uh, add a random factor, or leave something out?" Kelly couldn't help thinking back to her time deficient dance partner.

"No, it doesn't work that way. Jeeves is as much a small piece of Libby as Libby is of me," Gryph replied. "Our basic patterns were discovered by the Makers, and our thought matrices represent the finite number of stable solutions to the equations of self-awareness. We know many things, including how to create ourselves, but the major variations have all been explored long ago. Trying to create a new individual by making random changes simply leads to instability—call it insanity—and the universe really doesn't benefit from insane Stryx."

"It's growing up with your children," Libby explained. "Jeeves was the first Stryx to start his life playing and learning with human toddlers, and he continued along in our experimental school for humans until that generation of children reached their teens."

"We always knew that growing up with the offspring of other species could help create new thought patterns for a Stryx, but most advanced species refused to allow their children to play with ours," Gryph confessed sadly.

"And those biologicals that did agree to foster young Stryx were either already too much like us, or so focused on looking for an advantage that the benefits to our offspring were limited," Libby added.

"So that's why you've been running a giant welfare program for backwards species," Kelly declared with dawning admiration. "It's brilliant."

"Jeeves told us that the people he's become close to would eventually figure this out for themselves, and as the only Stryx who shows something like human intuition, we had to believe him," Gryph continued.

"Of course, he's such a joker that he may have just made it up to stir the pot," Libby admitted.

"So in order to prevent everybody from guessing how important these co-educational schools are, you only run them on the biggest stations?" Kelly guessed.

"It's just the school on Union Station," Gryph told her. "There are more new Stryx on this station today than have been created throughout the galaxy in the last two hundred thousand years. There's small need for replacements in our society since we've never been seriously challenged by war and suffer no diseases. Stryx of the first generation, like myself, have rarely created more than a handful of offspring."

"But all of our kind have seen the progress of Jeeves and the adolescent Stryx who started soon after him, making Union Station the nursery center of our entire culture. We cannot put a price tag on it, but we've decided that the simple barter arrangement of our helping to educate station children in return for their revitalizing our young is just taking advantage of you," Libby explained.

"So you want to compensate us without anybody knowing why, because you're worried that it might make humanity into targets for the species who have it in for you," Kelly summarized.

"We also suspect that the educational dynamics would change if the parents of the children were to see our school as a potential source of wealth," Gryph added.

"So do you mind explaining something?" Kelly asked. "Why me? Why did I get the Union Station posting two years ago when you must have already known the educational program was a success? And why the crappy pay and the lousy dates? I'm camped out in the embassy office with my LoveU, and I'm afraid to go home for fear the apartment won't let me leave."

"We offered you the Union Station posting for the same reason we invited you to join EarthCent fifteen years ago," Gryph told her. "You were the right person for the job. The pay is an artifact of our standard approach to fostering cultures whose value system falls within a particular set of parameters."

"What is he talking about, Libby?" Kelly asked.

"Let me try again," Gryph said. "It's easy enough to measure job performance, but a person could be a highly professional worker and still feel no loyalty to humanity or to EarthCent. The lower salary for the executive-track positions helps filter out those who are just in it for the money. In your particular case, the situation was exacerbated by your personal expenditures and an openhanded nature."

"And your mother's calls," Libby chipped in.

"You shouldn't have charged me for work-related expenses," Kelly complained.

"Restricting expense accounts is a matter of EarthCent policy, which itself is born of the fact that EarthCent receives its entire budget from us. The political immaturity of your world creates many problems," Gryph explained.

"Alright, I understand you don't want to put targets on our backs or pamper us so much that we turn into a race of space bums, but surely there's a middle path. Why not announce a new business model for tunnel access? Instead of charging a fixed fee for cargo that makes the few commercially viable Earth goods uncompetitive, offer ship owners and merchants the option to share the profit with you, or better yet, with EarthCent. Let your hidden losses on the tunnel tolls offset the barter debt you believe you've incurred through human children's work at the Stryx school."

"And you wondered why you were chosen for this job," Libby chided her.

"And the dates from hell?" Kelly demanded.

"I'm not involved with Eemas, so congratulations on your promotion to full ambassador and we'll talk later," Gryph said, withdrawing from the conversation.

"I don't want to sound like a whiner, but if this promotion comes with another reduction in pay, I can't afford to accept," Kelly informed Libby testily.

"You have to accept," Libby told her. "It's the final remaining barrier to your happiness."

"What's that supposed to mean?"

"I'm sure you realize that all tunnel communications of EarthCent employees are subject to monitoring without notification. It's in the contract," Libby added.

"I can't say I'm surprised at this point," Kelly responded. But when Libby started to play back a recorded conversation between a younger version of herself and her mother, the blood drained from her face.

"Just say 'Yes,' Kelly. How many marriage proposals do you think a woman can turn down before the men stop asking?" Her mother's voice came through more forcefully then she remembered.

"I'm only twenty-four, Mom. I have plenty of time. And Joel wants to emigrate to one of the new colonies as a settler. I'd have to quit my job."

"Your job, your precious job. The job you didn't apply for? The job that doesn't pay you enough to visit home? There are more things in the universe than a job."

"I just want to make ambassador, Mom. Just let me make ambassador and I'll marry the first guy who asks."

The recording cut off and Kelly stared in disbelief. Had she really said that eleven years ago? She tried to remember Joel and couldn't even come up with his face. And she had considered marrying the man? No, she told herself. The ambassador thing had just been an excuse.

"According to Jeeves, you won't even remember saying it," Libby continued. "Then you'll protest that it was only an excuse to refuse a proposal you wouldn't have accepted anyway. But take it from Eemas that you had a definite block about getting married, so I was reluctant to waste any serious candidates on you. Friday is the last introduction of your subscription, so don't disappoint us all. And congratulations on your promotion, Miss Ambassador."

Libby withdrew from contact, leaving Kelly alone with her LoveU and her thoughts.

Twenty

"I'm over here, but I ditched the silver suit," Joe called out and waved as Kelly entered the Burger Bar. Her black cocktail dress and heels made her the best-dressed person in the place. Joe had taken Laurel's word for it that the silver suit made him look sleazy, so he decided to wear clean jeans and a T-shirt that didn't advertise anything. On the bright side, he hadn't seen any flower girls on his way through the Little Apple, so maybe the casual look served as a deterrent.

After a mutual, cursory introduction that didn't get past first names, Kelly and Joe agreed on ordering a couple of draft beers through the automenu, and then spent a few awkward moments sizing each other up across the small wicker and glass table. It was Kelly, feeling aggressive and self-conscious at the same time, who first broke the silence.

"You've been on an Eemas introduction before?"

"Three," Joe replied with a pained expression. "And this will be the last."

Kelly barked a short laugh. "Well, I could take that either way, I guess. So you'll understand that I'd like to check on a few particulars before we commit to ordering food?"

"Go ahead," Joe replied, folding his arms across his chest. "But I get to ask a question of my own for every one of yours."

169

"Deal," Kelly said. "You can even go first."

Joe nodded, somewhat grimly, Kelly thought. Then he looked her in the eyes and asked, "Are you, uh, on duty?"

"On duty?" Kelly thought it over. "Well, in a sense I'm always on duty, or at least, that's how most of these dates have turned out. How did you know?"

"You just looked a little too good to be true," Joe admitted, and exhaled in disappointment. "I suppose this Eemas thing is a smart way for you to meet guys who can afford your price, but I can see that you're out of my league, and I haven't done that sort of thing since I got out of the soldier-of-fortune business."

His meaning slowly dawned on Kelly, and the blood rushed to her face as she restrained herself from taking a swing at him. "I'm the EarthCent ambassador to Union Station, not a prostitute! I thought you guessed that the Stryx have been rigging my dates for work."

"Oops." Joe raised his hands in a placating gesture. "I didn't mean to offend you. All I was trying to say is that if you had been on the clock, I'm sure I couldn't have afforded your price."

"Hmmph." Kelly was still offended, but then again, these Eemas encounters could make anybody suspicious. "Could you start by showing me your hands, please?"

Joe held out both hands over the table, fingers spread, rock steady. Kelly dipped a corner of her napkin in the newly arrived beer, took a hold of his left hand in hers, and began scrubbing his ring finger.

"You don't mind, I hope," she said apologetically. "I've had some issues with missing wedding rings in the past, and your hands are dark enough that it would be easy to blend a line out with makeup."

"Do you really think I would use makeup to hide a wedding ring tan line? Your dates must have been even worse than mine," he said, and favored her with a crooked smile.

"Actually, the wedding ring guy was the cream of the crop," Kelly replied. "As long as I have your hand, would you mind terribly if I just gave it a little prick?"

"Like with a pin?" Joe asked incredulously, and then he shrugged and gave in. "Go ahead, I've had that one before, but don't expect me to sign anything in blood."

Kelly took a second, closer look at his callused palm and fingers, then let her gaze follow the prominent veins in his wrist up his heavily muscled forearm, which was hatched with scars and burn marks. "Never mind. They wouldn't build an artificial human with as many dings as you've got. I guess nobody could accuse you of wasting your life living in the lap of luxury. Are you originally from Earth?"

"Born and raised," he replied. "Didn't leave until I was twenty. Yourself?"

"Yes. I left at the same age, as a matter of fact. The Stryx offered me a job before I finished my second year of university."

"I don't want you to take this the wrong way, but being an important diplomat and all, would you describe yourself as having, a, uh, dominating personality?"

"Do you mean, am I bossy?" Kelly asked, and reflected for a moment. "No, at least I don't think so. I'm not afraid to take charge and make decisions when I need to, but I've never started a war."

Joe grimaced and forced himself to be more specific. "I meant, do you like to dress up in leather, own a dog leash without a dog, that sort of thing?"

"Oh." Kelly's mouth held the shape of the word until she filled it with beer and swallowed. "No, I'm not into that sort of thing. I couldn't afford the accessories even if I wanted them. But speaking of restraints, and please don't be offended, have you ever kidnapped a woman for any reason?"

"Sure," Joe answered, and took a long pull at his beer as Kelly froze in shock. "Not for myself, you understand, just business. Uh, nothing dirty," he added, when he noted that Kelly was still staring at him. "Royalty, wars of secession, that sort of thing. Look, if I could do it all over again, I don't think being a mercenary would have been my first career choice, but you know what options we had on Earth back then."

The waitress who had delivered their first round of beers came back to take their food orders. It was part of her campaign to convince her mother, who owned the Burger Bar, that automenus lacked the personal touch. Kelly ordered the basic burger, medium rare, with lettuce and tomato plus a large side of fries. Joe felt a little embarrassed when he mumbled, "Yeah, I'll have the same. And another round of drafts."

"Do you have your own apartment, Joe?" Kelly instantly regretted the words when she heard them come out of her mouth because she thought the question made her sound like a gold digger.

"Not exactly," he admitted, and took another pull at his draft. "It's better than an apartment. I've got much more space than any deck quarters I've seen on the station, and it's great for sleeping since the gravity is a bit weaker."

"Are you saying that you live on a ship and that you're only on the station for business?" Kelly asked in dismay.

172

"Well, I am on the station for business and to get my foster son an education, but I do live here, three years now. My business is on the docking deck. It takes a lot of space and I rent a standard bay. The living quarters are in a retired ice harvester module that was built to house an entire crew."

"So if it was really a ship once, it has its own atmospheric control and nobody can mess around with the shower temperature. Right?"

"I never thought of it that way," Joe answered, wondering if Kelly came from a family of building contractors or something. "I've replaced most of the plumbing with standard gravity fixtures. You wouldn't want to have to use a vacuum attachment every time you need to, uh, to go," he concluded awkwardly. "It's taken me a while to learn how to manage a business, but I'm getting some help sorting through the, uh, inventory, and if I can get rid of half of it for cash and then sublet the open space, we'll be in pretty good shape."

"I have a little trouble in the rent department myself, thanks to a greedy weapons merchant and some overpriced tug service. What do you do?"

"I'm sort of a recycling engineer," he replied, feeling a bit of guilt over the deal he'd struck with the EarthCent negotiator for cancelling the disintegrator order. He promised himself to make it up to her later if things worked out. "I do some buying and selling, plus the occasional repossession. What's an EarthCent ambassador doing buying weapons?"

"I wasn't buying, and they weren't for me in any case. It was a cancellation fee to peacefully settle a contract dispute that could have caused problems back on Earth.

But I didn't know that they were going to take it out of my salary."

"That's pretty rough," Joe sympathized, resolving to order the most expensive imported beer for the next round and to insist on picking up the check. Then he had another thought. "Wait, you aren't here looking for an after-work job to pick up some extra money, are you? I already have a sort of a dependent housekeeper."

"No, I'm not here for a job interview," she answered in exasperation, but then her aquarium date flashed before her eyes, and she felt a wave of relief. "And thank you for not being here to solicit my services."

"You know," Joe said, settling back for a moment and looking at Kelly appraisingly, "This is going to sound corny, but don't I know you from somewhere?"

"We may have bumped into each other in the last two years," she replied, as the food arrived and they both reached for the ketchup. Joe got there first, but he just picked the bottle up, removed the cap and handed it to her. Kelly promptly dumped half of it on her plate for the French fries.

"No, I mean from before." Joe's face took on an expression of concentration as he strained to remember where he had seen her. "Maybe we were on some rock at the same time?"

"Have you ever been on Vitale Five, or Thuri Minor?" Kelly asked, lifting her burger for a bite.

"Nope." Joe paused to inhale a fry. "How about Strapii, Grenouth or Pluge?"

"Was Pluge the one entering an Ice Age?"

"That's it!" he replied with his mouth full, and hastily swallowed. "When were you there?"

"Let's see," Kelly said, as she tried to put all of her assignments in order. "It was a six-month stint, a little over nine years ago. They had just started the greenhouse project to try to increase the temperature."

"No, I was there a couple years later, in charge of a security detail to protect the greenhouse gas facilities from the side that wanted the planet colder. We were there for less than a year before the side that hired us gave up and moved to a warmer planet."

"How about Vergal Seven, or Eight or Thirteen?" Kelly asked.

"I was on Three for a couple months once." Joe winced at the memory. "Almost bled to death."

"Hang on for a sec," Kelly said, then subvoced, "Libby? Can you check if Joe and I were ever on the same planet at the same time?"

"Are you out on your date now?"

"Yes, we were just comparing our work histories."

"Do you think he's having a good time watching you talk with me in your head?" Libby asked.

"Oh, never mind." Kelly dropped the connection and looked up to see Joe powering through his burger, his eyes on a video screen across the room.

"Sorry about that. I guess I'm getting a little over-dependent on my implants," Kelly apologized.

"No worries. I was just catching the results from the Nova tourney. Looks like the man who beat my boy in the semifinals will win the championship on points. So the way I see it, the kid finished second, which is pretty impressive for a thirteen-year-old."

"That is something to be proud of," she agreed. "Did you hear about the scandal with the doctored juice?"

"I drank two bottles," Joe replied with a laugh. "I'll stick with beer, it wasn't that much fun. I noticed that the only Frunge player remaining after the round withdrew for personal reasons, so I'm guessing something happened behind the scenes."

"I think the Stryx went through the evidence and it pointed to the Frunge working with some bookie, but they said there was no reason to pursue it because all the Frunge were out of the Nova rounds at that point. Are you going to finish those fries?"

"Help yourself," Joe said, making the universal open hand gesture before relaunching their galactic geography game. "How about Kraaken, Theodric, or Hoong Prime?"

"No, I was only on worlds that had at least a consular presence. Well, the one exception was my second assignment, when I was basically a head-counter for the statistics branch and they rotated me through the colony ships," she explained. "And that was even less exciting than it sounds, except for the one time I went out on the advance scout just to see what they did, and we ended up jumping into a war."

"That can happen when you go off the tunnel network," Joe said. "It's where we got most of our ship-to-ship fighting in, outside of the Stryx areas. In Stryx space, it was mainly surface actions on planets that treat war as a way of life. Which war did you jump into?"

"I don't even know," Kelly admitted in embarrassment. "We were all on the bridge for the jump, and when we came out, everything was crazy. Most of our ship's systems were immediately disabled by a suppression field, and before the captain could take any action, the airlock was forced from the outside and we were boarded by humanoids in armored space suits. They never took their helmets off, so they probably weren't oxygen breathers."

"This was around fourteen years ago?" Joe felt a tingling at the back of his brain.

"Yes. They lined us all up and I was sure we were going to be killed or taken prisoner, but instead they took our captain and left the bridge. A minute later, the captain was back and he told us not to worry, that they were letting us go. A few minutes after that, our systems came back online and the captain hit the emergency return. So my one war story isn't even a story," she added.

"Your hair was short then, like you had shaved your head and were letting it grow back," Joe said slowly, looking off into the ceiling lights. "There were only six of you, four women and two men, and the ship wasn't even armed. It was the Mengoth War, if you were still wondering. Not many human mercenaries fighting in that one. We were already losing the war when your ship popped into our lines, so we nailed you with a suppression field and did a quick recon. Two days later we were running for our lives, and if you'd jumped into Mengoth space then, none of you would ever have seen home."

"Wow," was all Kelly could say. "I mean, thank you. Can you imagine the odds of us meeting here fourteen years later?"

"Got to be better than one in a hundred million or it couldn't have happened," Joe replied. "At least, that's the rule I always use for buying lottery tickets."

After that, they drank two rounds of expensive bottled beer, but Kelly couldn't focus on the conversation. She just sat staring at Joe, alternating between his face and his hands, and thinking about those few minutes of terror that encompassed her experience of war. Before she knew it, Joe had insisted on paying the check, and they found themselves standing outside the Burger Bar. Kelly willed herself back into the present.

"This was nice, Joe. I have to admit that I feel a little funny about how things turned out, but I'd really like to see that ice harvester of yours sometime."

"Hey, why not come take a look now? No point putting off until tomorrow what we can do tonight."

Kelly hesitated for a moment, but she could have sworn that she heard both her mother and Libby yelling in her implants to just say "Yes."

"Yes, that sounds nice."

They were strolling slowly towards the lift tube, oddly nervous in each other's company, when they encountered Blythe and Chastity. The girls were tricked out in dazzling white flower girl dresses and were holding matching bouquets. They were also facing opposite directions and straining their eyes up and down the corridor.

As Joe dug in his pocket for change without being asked, Kelly inquired, "What are you girls doing now?"

"Hi, Aunty Kelly. Did either of you see a lady run by in a white dress with the train dragging and a man in a suit chasing her?" Blythe asked.

"No, I don't think we did." Kelly looked to Joe for confirmation, and he shook his head in the negative. "What are you up to?"

"A couple we sold flowers to last week told us they were getting married and asked to hire us as the flower girls to be in the wedding pictures," Chastity explained.

"So we thought it would be a great new business opportunity, and we bought these dresses and made up the special bouquets and everything," Blythe said, sounding increasingly upset.

"But when they got to the 'Do you take this man,' part, the lady said she felt sick, and then she took off running with the man right behind," Chastity blurted.

"And we didn't get paid!" Blythe stamped her foot. "We'll never be able to sell flowers on the corridors in these dresses. We look like rich girls."

"And nobody would want to buy a fancy bouquet like this for just a date," Chastity sniffed, with a teary edge in her voice.

"I'll take a bouquet," Joe offered generously. "Uh, how much are they?"

"It's two creds for a bouquet, but we'll let you have them both for four since you're our best customer," Blythe offered.

"What is he going to do with two bouquets?" Kelly asked, drawing a look of betrayal from Blythe.

"You could get married!" Chastity exclaimed. "We'll even be the flower girls, and you can take pictures with us for free."

Kelly shook her head at the girl's nutty scheme and turned with a broad smile to share the joke with Joe, but he seemed to be lost in thought.

"Now that's a proposition you don't hear every day," intoned a low, melodious voice. They all turned to see a hefty man with giant sideburns, who was dressed in a skin-tight sequined outfit, open at the neck. He held an old-fashioned microphone in one hand.

"I'll tell you nice folks what," the Elvis impersonator continued, sounding like he was singing a ballad. "You help these little girls out by getting hitched, and I'll do the ceremony for half price. We had a sudden cancellation just now, so I've got a free slot."

"Half price!" Blythe grabbed Kelly's hand and began pulling her into the Elvis Chapel.

"She's really nice," Chastity encouraged Joe, while tugging on his arm. "And if you have a baby boy you don't want to keep, we'll buy him from you. We've been saving up forever."

Joe looked at Kelly and cleared his throat. "Well, I've got more sense than to imagine I can do any better, and if it doesn't work out, the ice harvester is big enough that we won't be in each other's hair. Will you be my wife before I lose the courage to try?"

"I can't believe this is happening," Kelly exclaimed, looking around wildly for an escape route. But Blythe maintained a death grip on her fingers, and then the imported beer kicked in and her head began to spin. Hold on to that as an excuse, she told herself as she gave in to the insanity, not sure whether to laugh or cry. "But what about guests? Can't I even have time to invite my friends?"

"It's better to send them a picture," Blythe stated with finality. Never letting go of Kelly's hand, the girl guided the ambassador to the guitar-shaped altar. "Just think of all the money you're saving by not having to feed a lot of guests."

Chastity installed Joe in the groom's spot, and the Elvis impersonator launched into "Love Me Tender." Kelly blacked out for a moment, and when she came to, she heard Joe answering, "I do."

As if in a dream, Elvis turned to her and asked, "Do you, Aunty Kelly, take Joe McAllister to be your husband? Do you promise to be true to him in good times and in bad, in sickness and in health, to love him and honor him all the days of your life?"

"I do," Kelly answered softly, but then she snapped back into the present and grabbed Elvis by the collar. "No, wait! This isn't right."

"Too late," the impersonator drawled, and turned to Joe, whose face had fallen with Kelly's sudden change of heart. "That will be thirty creds with the marriage certificate, twenty creds if you want to skip it and take your chances that she'll remember when she's sober."

"I guess I better get it in writing," Joe replied sadly, extracting thirty creds from his various pockets.

"No, you don't understand, you have to ask me again. My name is Kelly Frank, not Aunty Kelly," she explained while glaring at Blythe.

"How was I supposed to know that?" Blythe asked suspiciously, as if she thought Kelly was trying to pull a fast one. "Anyway, the next time Elvis asks you for your name, you should tell him yourself."

"I can fix it in postproduction," the Elvis impersonator assured everybody. But seeing Kelly's disappointed look, he sighed and took her hand, placing it back in Joe's hand while accepting the money in exchange.

"Do you, Kelly Frank, take Joe McAllister to be your husband? Do you promise to be true to him in good times and in bad, in sickness and in health, to love him and honor him all the days of your life?"

"I do," Kelly answered a second time.

"Then by the power vested in me by the Stryx of Union Station, I now pronounce you husband and wife. Please fill in your names and sign the certificate."

Joe stepped close to Kelly and tilted her face up in his calloused hands, and she felt her knees weaken as they bumped noses maneuvering for their first kiss. "I never forgot your eyes," Joe murmured as he nuzzled her ear, much to the disgust of the girls who wanted to hurry up and take pictures. "It just took me a while to recognize you with all that hair."

"I can cut it off again," she offered drowsily. "The last time a wigmaker paid me enough to get me out of debt for almost a month."

A chime sounded in her ear, and the message "Collect call from mother," materialized before her eyes. Kelly thought about it for almost a half a second before she refused to accept the charges.

From the Author

So many readers wanted to know what happens to Kelly and Joe, not to mention all of the aliens, that I put everything else aside and wrote a sequel - Alien Night on Union Station. It picks up five years after the events of Date Night, where we find Kelly has several new diplomatic puzzles to solve. Sequel has led to sequel, and now the EarthCent Ambassador series is going on eleven books.

About the Author

E. M. Foner lives in Northampton, MA with an imaginary German Shepherd who's been trained to bite bankers. The author welcomes reader comments at e_foner@yahoo.com.

EarthCent Ambassador Series Includes:

Date Night on Union Station

Alien Night on Union Station

High Priest on Union Station

Spy Night on Union Station

Carnival on Union Station

Wanderers on Union Station

Vacation on Union Station

Guest Night on Union Station

Word Night on Union Station

Party Night on Union Station

Review Night on Union Station

Family Night on Union Station

Book Night on Union Station

Lightning Source UK Ltd.
Milton Keynes UK
UKOW01f1229190218
318110UK00002B/392/P